Read ALL

T0228665

continued . . .

THE CAT WHO ROBBED A BANK: As the Highland Games approach, Qwill tries to make sense of Koko's sudden interest in photographs, pennies, and paper towels . . .

THE CAT WHO SMELLED A RAT: A drought plagues Moose County—and a bewildering murder case plagues Qwill and the cats . . .

THE CAT WHO WENT UP THE CREEK: While visiting Black Creek, Qwill and the cats must solve the murder of a drowned man before they're up the creek without a paddle . . .

THE CAT WHO BROUGHT DOWN THE HOUSE: Koko's stage debut is postponed when Qwill suspects the cat's costar may be guilty of murder . . .

THE CAT WHO TALKED TURKEY: A body's been found on Qwill's property, and now he and the cats will have to determine who committed this fowl deed . . .

THE CAT WHO WENT BANANAS: Koko finds a bunch of clues when an out-of-town actor dies mysteriously . . .

THE CAT WHO DROPPED A BOMBSHELL: As Pickax plans its big parade, Qwill and the cats cope with an approaching storm—and two suspicious deaths . . .

THE CAT WHO HAD 60 WHISKERS: News of a fatal bee sting has Koko's whiskers twitching—and Qwill itching to find out more . . .

And don't miss . . .

THE CAT WHO HAD 14 TALES
A delightful collection of feline mystery fiction!

SHORT AND TALL TALES: LEGENDS OF MOOSE COUNTY
Legends, stories, and anecdotes from four hundred miles north of everywhere . . .

THE PRIVATE LIFE OF THE CAT WHO . . .
A charming collection of feline antics that provides an intimate look at the private lives of those extraordinary Siamese cats Koko and Yum Yum.

Titles by Lilian Jackson Braun

THE CAT WHO COULD READ BACKWARDS
THE CAT WHO ATE DANISH MODERN
THE CAT WHO TURNED ON AND OFF
THE CAT WHO SAW RED
THE CAT WHO PLAYED BRAHMS
THE CAT WHO PLAYED POST OFFICE
THE CAT WHO KNEW SHAKESPEARE
THE CAT WHO SNIFFED GLUE
THE CAT WHO WENT UNDERGROUND
THE CAT WHO TALKED TO GHOSTS
THE CAT WHO LIVED HIGH
THE CAT WHO KNEW A CARDINAL
THE CAT WHO MOVED A MOUNTAIN
THE CAT WHO WASN'T THERE
THE CAT WHO WENT INTO THE CLOSET
THE CAT WHO CAME TO BREAKFAST
THE CAT WHO BLEW THE WHISTLE
THE CAT WHO SAID CHEESE
THE CAT WHO TAILED A THIEF
THE CAT WHO SANG FOR THE BIRDS
THE CAT WHO SAW STARS
THE CAT WHO ROBBED A BANK
THE CAT WHO SMELLED A RAT
THE CAT WHO WENT UP THE CREEK
THE CAT WHO BROUGHT DOWN THE HOUSE
THE CAT WHO TALKED TURKEY
THE CAT WHO WENT BANANAS
THE CAT WHO DROPPED A BOMBSHELL
THE CAT WHO HAD 60 WHISKERS

SHORT STORY COLLECTIONS:
THE CAT WHO HAD 14 TALES
SHORT & TALL TALES
THE PRIVATE LIFE OF THE CAT WHO...

Lilian Jackson Braun

The Cat Who Had 14 Tales

J

JOVE BOOKS, NEW YORK

THE BERKLEY PUBLISHING GROUP
Published by the Penguin Group
Penguin Group (USA) Inc.
375 Hudson Street, New York, New York 10014, USA
Penguin Group (Canada), 90 Eglinton Avenue East, Suite 700, Toronto, Ontario M4P 2Y3, Canada
(a division of Pearson Penguin Canada Inc.)
Penguin Books Ltd., 80 Strand, London WC2R 0RL, England
Penguin Group Ireland, 25 St. Stephen's Green, Dublin 2, Ireland (a division of Penguin Books Ltd.)
Penguin Group (Australia), 250 Camberwell Road, Camberwell, Victoria 3124, Australia
(a division of Pearson Australia Group Pty. Ltd.)
Penguin Books India Pvt. Ltd., 11 Community Centre, Panchsheel Park, New Delhi—110 017, India
Penguin Group (NZ), 67 Apollo Drive, Rosedale, North Shore 0745, Auckland, New Zealand
(a division of Pearson New Zealand Ltd.)
Penguin Books (South Africa) (Pty.) Ltd., 24 Sturdee Avenue, Rosebank, Johannesburg 2196,
South Africa

Penguin Books Ltd., Registered Offices: 80 Strand, London WC2R 0RL, England

This is a work of fiction. Names, characters, places, and incidents either are the product of the author's imagination or are used fictitiously, and any resemblance to actual persons, living or dead, business establishments, events, or locales is entirely coincidental. The publisher does not have any control over and does not assume any responsibility for author or third-party websites or their content.

"Phut Phat Concentrates" was first published in *Ellery Queen's Mystery Magazine*, December 1963.
"The Dark One" was first published in *Ellery Queen's Mystery Magazine*, July 1966.
"SuSu and the 8:30 Ghost" was first published in *Ellery Queen's Mystery Magazine*, April 1964.
"The Sin of Madame Phloi" was first published in *Ellery Queen's Mystery Magazine*, June 1962.
"Tragedy on New Year's Eve" was first published in *Ellery Queen's Mystery Magazine*, March 1968.

THE CAT WHO HAD 14 TALES

A Jove Book / published by arrangement with the author

PRINTING HISTORY
First Jove mass-market edition / March 1988

Copyright © 1988 by Lilian Jackson Braun.
Cover design by Elaine Groh.
Cover photo of flashlight © Brand X Pictures/Fotosearch.
Cover photo of wedding bands © PhotoDisc/Fotosearch.
Cover photo of tieback sash cords © Ingram Publishing/Fotosearch.
Cover photo of jigsaw puzzle © PureStock/Fotosearch.

ISBN: 978-0-515-09497-8

JOVE®
Jove Books are published by The Berkley Publishing Group,
a division of Penguin Group (USA) Inc.,
375 Hudson Street, New York, New York 10014.
JOVE is a registered trademark of Penguin Group (USA) Inc.
The "J" design is a trademark belonging to Penguin Group (USA) Inc.

PRINTED IN THE UNITED STATES OF AMERICA

43 42 41 40 39 38 37 36 35

CONTENTS

Phut Phat Concentrates

Phut Phat knew, at an early age, that humans were an inferior breed. They were unable to see in the dark. They ate and drank unthinkable concoctions. And they had only five senses; the pair who lived with Phut Phat could not even transmit their thoughts without resorting to words.

For more than a year, ever since arriving at the townhouse, Phut Phat had been trying to intro-

"Phut Phat Concentrates" was first published in *Ellery Queen's Mystery Magazine*, December 1963.

duce his system of communication, but his two pupils had made scant progress. At dinnertime he would sit in a corner, concentrating, and suddenly they would say: "Time to feed the cat," as if it were their own idea.

Their ability to grasp Phut Phat's messages extended only to the bare necessities of daily living, however.

Beyond that, nothing ever got through to them, and it seemed unlikely they would ever increase their powers.

Nevertheless, life in the townhouse was comfortable enough. It followed a fairly dependable routine, and to Phut Phat routine was the greatest of all goals. He deplored such deviations as tardy meals, loud noises, unexplained persons on the premises, or liver during the week. He always had liver on Sunday.

It was a fashionable part of the city in which Phut Phat lived. The three-story brick townhouse was furnished with thick rugs and down-cushioned chairs and tall pieces of furniture from which he could look down on questionable visitors. He could rise to the top of a high-boy in a single leap, and when he scampered from first-floor kitchen to second-floor living room to third-floor bedroom, his ascent up the carpeted staircase was very close to flight, for

Phut Phat was a Siamese. His fawn-colored coat was finer than ermine. His eight seal brown points (there had been nine before that trip to the hospital) were as sleek as panne velvet, and his slanted eyes brimmed with a mysterious blue.

Those who lived with Phut Phat in the townhouse were identified in his consciousness as ONE and TWO. It was ONE who supplied the creature comforts, fed his vanity with lavish compliments, and sometimes adorned his throat with jeweled collars taken from her own wrists.

TWO, on the other hand, was valued chiefly for games and entertainment. He said very little, but he jingled keys at the end of a shiny chain and swung them back and forth for Phut Phat's amusement. And every morning in the dressing room he swished a necktie in tantalizing arcs while Phut Phat leaped and grabbed with pearly claws.

These daily romps, naps on downy cushions, outings in the coop on the fire escape, and two meals a day constituted the pattern of Phut Phat's life.

Then one Sunday he sensed a disturbing lapse in the household routine. The Sunday papers, usually scattered on the library floor for him to shred with his claws, were stacked neatly on the desk. Furniture was rearranged. The house was filled with flowers, which he was not allowed to chew. ONE was nervous, and TWO was too busy to play. A stranger in a white coat arrived and clattered glassware, and when Phut Phat investigated an aroma of shrimp and smoked oysters in the kitchen, the maid shooed him away.

Phut Phat seemed to be in everyone's way. Finally he was deposited in his wire coop on the fire escape, where he watched sparrows in the garden below until his stomach felt empty. Then he howled to come indoors.

He found ONE at her dressing table, fussing with her hair and unmindful of his hunger. Hopping lightly to the table, he sat erect among the sparkling bottles, stiffened his tail, and fastened his blue eyes on ONE's forehead. In that attitude he proceeded to concentrate— and concentrate—and concentrate. It was never easy to communicate with ONE. Her mind hopped about like a sparrow, never relaxed, and Phut Phat had to strain every nerve to convey his meaning.

Suddenly ONE darted a look in his direction. A thought had occurred to her.

"Oh, John," she called to TWO, who was

brushing his teeth, "would you ask Millie to feed Phuffy. I forgot his dinner until this very minute. It's after five o'clock and I haven't fixed my hair yet. You'd better put your coat on; people will start coming soon. And please tell Howard to light the candles. You might stack some records on the stereo, too. . . . No, wait a minute. If Millie is still working on the hors d'oeuvres, would you feed Phuffy yourself? Just open a can of anything."

At this, Phut Phat stared at ONE with an intensity that made his thought waves almost visible.

"Oh, John, I forgot," she corrected. "It's Sunday, and he'll expect liver. But before you do that, would you zip the back of my dress and put my emerald bracelet on Phuffy? Or maybe I'll wear the emerald myself, and he can have the amethyst . . . John! Do you realize it's five-fifteen! I wish you'd put your coat on."

"And I wish you'd simmer down," said TWO. "No one ever comes at the stated hour. Why do you insist on giving big parties, Helen, if it makes you so nervous?"

"Nervous? I'm not nervous. Besides, it was *your* idea to invite your clients and my friends at the same time. You said we should kill a

5

whole blasted flock of birds with one blasted stone. . . . Now, *please*. John, are you going to feed Phuffy? He's staring at me and making my head ache."

Phut Phat scarcely had time to swallow his creamed liver, wash his face, and arrange himself on the living room mantel before people started to arrive. His irritation at the disrupted routine was lessened somewhat by the prospect of being admired by the guests. His name meant "beautiful" in Siamese, and he was well aware of his pulchritude. Lounging between a pair of Georgian silver candlesticks, with one foreleg extended and the other exquisitely bent under at the ankle, with his head erect and gaze withdrawn, with his tail drooping nonchalantly over the edge of the marble mantel, he awaited compliments.

It was a large party, and Phut Phat observed that very few of the guests knew how to pay their respects to a cat. Some talked nonsense in a false voice. Others made startling movements in his direction, or worse still, tried to pick him up.

There was one knowledgeable man, however, who approached with the proper attitude of deference and reserve. Phut Phat squeezed his eyes in appreciation. The admirer was a distin-

guished-looking man who leaned heavily on a
shiny stick. Standing at a respectful distance, he
slowly held out his hand with one finger extended, and Phut Phat twitched his whiskers
politely.

"You are a living sculpture," said the man.

"That's Phut Phat," said ONE, who had
pushed through the crowded room toward the
fireplace. "He's the head of our household."

"He is obviously of excellent stock," said the
man with the shiny cane, addressing his hostess
in the same courtly manner that had charmed
Phut Phat.

"Yes, he could probably win ribbons if we
wanted to enter him in shows, but he's strictly
a pet. He never goes out except in his coop on
the fire escape."

"A splendid idea!" said the guest. "I should
like such an arrangement for my own cat. She's
a tortoiseshell longhair. May I inspect this coop
before I leave?"

"Certainly. It's just outside the library window."

"You have a most attractive house."

"Thank you. We've been accused of decorat-
ing it to complement Phut Phat's coloring,
which is somewhat true. You'll notice we have

no breakable bric-a-brac. When he flies through the air, he recognizes no obstacles."

"Indeed, I have noticed you collect Georgian silver," the man said. "You have some fine examples."

"Apparently you know silver. Your cane is a rare piece."

He frowned in self-pity. "An attempt to extract a little pleasure from a sorry necessity." He hobbled a step or two.

"Would you like to see my silver collection downstairs in the dining room?" asked ONE. "All early examples, around the time of Wren."

Phut Phat, aware that the conversation no longer centered on his superlative qualities, jumped down from the mantel and stalked out of the room with several irritable flicks of the tail. He found an olive and pushed it down the heat register. Several feet stepped on him. In desperation he went upstairs to the guest room, where he discovered a mound of sable and mink and went to sleep.

After this upset in the household routine Phut Phat needed several days to catch up on his rest, so the coming week was a sleepy blur. But soon it was Sunday again, with creamed liver for breakfast, Sunday papers scattered over the floor, and everyone lounging around being pleasantly routine.

"Phuffy! Don't roll on those newspapers," said ONE. "John, the ink rubs off on his fur. Give him the *Wall Street Journal*; it's cleaner."

"Maybe he'd like to go out into his coop and get some sun."

"That reminds me, dear. Who was that charming man with the silver cane at our party? I didn't catch his name."

"I don't know," said TWO. "I thought he was someone you invited."

"Well, he must have come with one of the other guests. At any rate, he was interested in getting a coop like ours. He has a long-haired torty. And did I tell you the Hendersons have two Burmese kittens? They want us to go over and see them next Sunday and have a drink."

Another week passed, during which Phut Phat discovered a new perch. He found he could jump to the top of an antique armoire—a towering piece of furniture in the hall outside the library. Otherwise it was a routine week, followed by a routine weekend, and Phut Phat was content.

ONE and TWO were going out on Sunday evening to see the Burmese kittens, so Phut

Phat was served an early dinner, after which he fell asleep on the library sofa.

When the telephone rang and waked him, it was dark and he was alone. He raised his head and chattered at the instrument until it stopped its noise. Then he went back to sleep, chin on paw.

The second time the telephone started ringing, Phut Phat stood up and scolded it, arching his body in a vertical stretch and making a question mark with his tail. To express his annoyance he hopped on the desk and sharpened his claws on *Webster's Unabridged*. Then he spent quite some time chewing on a leather bookmark. After that he felt thirsty. He sauntered toward the powder room for a drink.

No lights were on, and no moonlight came through the windows, yet he moved through the dark rooms with assurance, sidestepping table legs and stopping to examine infinitesimal particles on the hall carpet. Nothing escaped his attention.

Phut Phat was lapping water, the tip of his tail was waving rapturously, when something caused him to raise his head and listen. His tail froze. Sparrows in the backyard? Rain on the fire escape? There was silence again. He lowered his head and resumed his drinking.

A second time he was alerted. Something was happening that was not routine. His tail bushed like a squirrel's, and with his whiskers full of alarm he stepped noiselessly into the hall, peering toward the library.

Someone was on the fire escape. Something was gnawing at the library window.

Petrified, he watched—until the window opened and a dark figure slipped into the room. With one lightning glide Phut Phat sprang to the top of the tall armoire.

There on his high perch, able to look down on the scene, he felt safe. But was it enough to feel safe? His ancestors had been watch-cats in Oriental temples centuries before. They had hidden in the shadows and crouched on high walls, ready to spring on any intruder and tear his face to ribbons—just as Phut Phat shredded the Sunday paper. A primitive instinct rose in his breast, but quickly it was quelled by civilized inhibitions.

The figure in the window advanced stealthily toward the hall, and Phut Phat experienced a sense of the familiar. It was the man with the shiny stick. This time, though, his presence smelled sinister. A small blue light now glowed from the head of the cane, and instead of leaning on it, the man pointed it ahead to guide his way out of the library and toward the staircase. As the intruder passed the armoire, Phut Phat's fur rose to form a sharp ridge down his spine. Instinct said: "Spring at him!" But vague fears held him back.

With feline stealth the man moved downstairs, unaware of two glowing diamonds that watched him in the blackness, and Phut Phat soon heard noises in the dining room. He sensed evil. Safe on top of the armoire, he trembled.

When the man reappeared he was carrying a bulky load, which he took to the library window. Then he crept to the third floor, and there were muffled sounds in the bedroom. Phut Phat licked his nose in apprehension.

Now the man reappeared, following a pool of blue light. As he approached the armoire, Phut Phat shifted his feet, bracing himself against something invisible. He felt a powerful compulsion to attack, and yet a fearful dismay.

"Get him!" commanded a savage impulse within him.

"Stay!" warned the fright throbbing in his head.

"Get him! . . . Now . . . now . . . . . . *NOW!*"

Phut Phat Concentrates

Phut Phat sprang at the man's head, ripping with razor claws wherever they sank into flesh.

The hideous scream that came from the intruder was like an electric shock; it sent Phut Phat sailing through space—up the stairs—into the bedroom—under the bed.

For a long time he quaked uncontrollably, his mouth parched and his ears inside-out with horror at what had happened. There was something strange and wrong about it, although its meaning eluded him. Waiting for time to heal his confusion, he huddled there in darkness and privacy. Blood soiled his claws. He sniffed with distaste and finally was compelled to lick them clean.

He did it slowly and with repugnance. Then he tucked his paws under his warm body and waited.

When ONE and TWO came home, he sensed their arrival even before the taxicab door slammed. He should have bounded to meet them, but the experience had left him in a daze, quivering internally, weak and unsure. He heard the rattle of the front door lock, feet climbing the stairs, and the click of the light switch in the room where he waited in bewilderment under the bed.

13

ONE gasped, then shrieked. "John! Someone's been in this room. We've been robbed!"

TWO's voice was incredulous. "How do you know?"

"My jewel case! Look! It's open—and empty!"

TWO threw open a closet door. "Your furs are still here, Helen. What about money? Did you have any money in the house?"

"I never leave money around. But the silver! What about the silver? John, go down and see. I'm afraid to look . . . No! Wait a minute!" ONE's voice rose in panic. "Where's Phut Phat? What happened to Phut Phat?"

"I don't know," said TWO with alarm. "I haven't seen him since we came in."

They searched the house, calling his name— unaware, with their limited senses, that Phut Phat was right there under the bed, brooding over the upheaval in his small world, and now and then licking his claws.

When at last, crawling on their hands and knees, they spied two eyes glowing red under the bed, they drew him out gently. ONE hugged him with a rocking embrace and rubbed her face, wet and salty, on his fur, while TWO stood by, stroking him with a heavy hand. Comforted and reassured, Phut Phat stopped trembling. He tried to purr, but the shock had contracted his larynx.

ONE continued to hold Phut Phat in her arms—and he had no will to jump down—even after two strange men were admitted to the house. They asked questions and examined all the rooms.

"Everything is insured," ONE told them, "but the silver is irreplaceable. It's old and very rare. Is there any chance of getting it back, Lieutenant?" She fingered Phut Phat's ears nervously.

"At this point it's hard to say," the detective said, "but you may be able to help us. Have you noticed any strange incidents lately? Any unusual telephone calls?"

"Yes," said ONE. "Several times recently the phone has rung, and when we answered it, no one was there."

"That's the usual method. They wait until they know you're not at home."

ONE gazed into Phut Phat's eyes. "Did the phone ring tonight while we were out, Phuffy?" she asked, shaking him lovingly. "If only Phut Phat could tell us what happened! He must have had a terrifying experience. Thank heaven he wasn't harmed."

Phut Phat raised his paw to lick between his toes, still defiled with human blood.

"If only Phuffy could tell us who was here!"

Phut Phat paused with toes spread and pink tongue extended. He stared at ONE's forehead.

"Have you folks noticed any strangers in the neighborhood?" the lieutenant was asking. "Anyone who would arouse suspicion?"

Phut Phat's body tensed, and his blue eyes, brimming with knowledge, bored into that spot above ONE's eyebrows.

"I can't think of anyone. Can you, John?"

TWO shook his head.

"Poor Phuffy," said ONE. "See how he stares at me; he must be hungry. Does Phuffy want a little snack?"

The cat squirmed.

"About those bloodstains on the windowsill," said the detective. "Would the cat attack anyone viciously enough to draw blood?"

"Heavens, no!" said ONE. "He's just a pampered little house pet. We found him hiding under the bed, scared stiff."

"And you're sure you can't remember any unusual incident lately? Has anyone come to the house who might have seen the silver or jewelry? Repairman? Window washer?"

"I wish I could be more helpful," said ONE, "but honestly, I can't think of a single suspect."

Phut Phat gave up!

Wriggling free, he jumped down from ONE's lap and walked toward the door with head depressed and hind legs stiff with disgust. He knew who it was. He knew! The man with the shiny stick. But it was useless to try to communicate. The human mind was so tightly closed that nothing important would ever penetrate. And ONE was so busy with her own chatter that her mind . . .

The jingle of keys caught Phut Phat's attention. He turned and saw TWO swinging his key chain back and forth, back and forth, and saying nothing. TWO always did more thinking than talking. Perhaps Phut Phat had been trying to communicate with the wrong mind. Perhaps TWO was really Number One in the household and ONE was Number Two.

Phut Phat froze in his position of concentration, sitting tall and compact with tail stiff. The key chain swung back and forth, and Phut Phat fastened his blue eyes on three wrinkles just underneath TWO's hairline. He concentrated. The key chain swung back and forth, back and forth. Phut Phat kept concentrating.

"Wait a minute," said TWO, coming out of

his puzzled silence. "I just thought of something. Helen, remember that party we gave a couple of weeks ago? There was one guest we couldn't account for—a man with a silver cane."

"Why, yes! He was curious about the coop on the fire escape. Why didn't I think of him? Lieutenant, he was terribly interested in our silver collection."

TWO said: "Does that suggest anything to you, Lieutenant?"

"Yes, it does." The detective exchanged nods with his partner.

"This man," ONE volunteered, "had a very cultivated voice and a charming manner. He walked with a limp."

"We know him," the detective said grimly. "The limp is phony. We know his method and what you tell us fits perfectly. But we didn't know he was operating in this neighborhood again."

ONE said: "What mystifies me is the blood on the windowsill."

Phut Phat arched his body in a long, luxurious stretch and walked from the room, looking for a soft, dark, quiet place. Now he would sleep. He felt relaxed and satisfied. He had made vital contact with a human mind, and perhaps—after all—there was hope. Some day they might learn the system, learn to open their minds and receive. They had a long way to go before they realized their potential. But there was hope.

Weekend of the
Big Puddle

Ghosts were no novelty to Percy. In England, his birthplace, they had them all the time. But British ghosts had always shown their good breeding; the uncouth pair that turned up at Percy's summer residence in Michigan left him outraged and chagrined.

Percy was a comfortable middle-aged bachelor with quiet tastes and fastidious habits, who distributed his contempt equally among small children, yipping dogs, and noisy adults. His own manners were impeccable, his reputation blameless. In fact, Percy would have been considered somewhat stuffy, had he been a man. Being a cat, he was admired for his good behavior.

He was a portly silver tabby with a gray-and-black coat patterned as precisely as a butterfly's wing. Something about his strong, fierce face gave an impression of integrity, rather like a benevolent man-eating tiger.

Percy spent summer weekends at a rustic chalet in the north woods—on the shore of the exclusive Big Pine Lake. Here he dozed away the hours in the company of Cornelius and Margaret or stared unblinking at the placid lake.

Cornelius was a comfortable middle-aged attorney with equally quiet tastes. He too was portly and had Percy's look of integrity. On weekends Cornelius worked jigsaw puzzles, took untaxing strolls with his wife, or went through the motions of fishing. Margaret knitted sweaters or puttered lovingly in the push-button kitchen. When they entertained, their guests were calm, temperate, and middle-aged, with no great desire to exert themselves. Everything was quite civilized and dull—the way

Percy liked it—until the weekend of the big puddle.

Bill Diddleton and his wife had been invited to spend Saturday and Sunday at the chalet. The bar was stocked with the expensive brands that Cornelius took pride in serving, and the refrigerator contained Margaret's specialties: shrimp bisque, veal in aspic, and blueberry buckle. Her chief delight was the feeding of guests; for Cornelius the greatest pleasure came when he tied on a chef's apron and broiled the steaks that he ordered from Texas.

"I wonder what Bill's new wife will be like," Margaret murmured over her knitting as they awaited the arrival of the Diddletons. "I hope she appreciates good food."

"A piece of this puzzle is missing," said Cornelius, frowning at a jigsaw version of the Mona Lisa.

"It's under your left foot, dear. Do you think Percy will object to Bill? He's rather a boisterous character."

At the sound of his name Percy raised his head. He noticed the ball of yarn unwinding, but it failed to tempt him. He never disturbed Margaret's knitting or Cornelius's jigsaw puzzles.

The man beamed a brotherly smile at the silver tabby. "Percy, the gentleman you are about to meet is an excellent client of mine, and we shall all endeavor to tolerate his bombast for thirty-six hours."

Percy squeezed his eyes in casual consent, but when the Diddletons arrived, shouting and squealing and creating a general uproar, he retired to the balcony where he could observe from a discreet distance.

The woman, small and nervous, spoke in a shrill voice, and Percy put her in the classification with small yipping dogs. Nevertheless, he stared in fascination at her jewelry, which flashed in the shafts of sunlight slanting into the chalet. The man was muscular, arrogant, and active, like some of the boxer dogs Percy had encountered. The silver tabby had strong opinions about that particular breed.

Upon entering the chalet Bill Diddleton caught sight of a horizontal beam spanning the living room, and he jumped up and hand-walked the length of it. The irregularity of this conduct made Percy squirm uncomfortably.

"Well, well!" said Cornelius in his best genial tone. "After that exhibition of athletic prowess I daresay you are ready for a drink, my boy. And what is Mrs. Diddleton's pleasure, may I ask?"

"Call me Deedee," she said.

"Indeed! So I shall. Now, might I offer you a fine eighteen-year-old Scotch?"

"I've got a better idea," said Bill. "Just show me the bar and I'll mix you a drink you'll never forget. Got any tomato juice?"

"Bill's famous for this cute drink," said his wife. "It's tomato juice, ginger ale, Scotch, and . . ." Rolling her eyes upward to recollect the fourth ingredient, she shrieked. A disembodied head with staring eyes was wedged between the balusters of the balcony railing.

"That's only our Percy," Margaret explained. "He's not as menacing as he looks."

"A cat! I can't stand cats!"

Percy sensed that the weekend was beginning poorly, and he was right. For lunch Margaret had planned a lobster soufflé, to be followed by her special salad that she prepared at the table, basking in the flattering comments of guests. On this occasion Bill Diddleton insisted, however, on presiding at the salad bowl.

"You sit down and take it easy, Meg honey," he said, "and I'll show you how the experts toss greens."

"Isn't it wonderful the way Bill takes over?" Deedee said. "He's a wonderful cook. He made one of his wonderful cakes for this weekend."

"I call it a Lucky Seven torte," Bill said. "Seven layers, with seven different kinds of booze. It has to ripen twenty-four hours before we can eat it. . . . What's the matter, Meg? Afraid of a few calories?"

"Not at all," said Margaret lightly. "It's just that I had planned—"

"Now let's get this straight, honey. I don't want you folks going to a lot of trouble. It was great of you to invite us up here, and we want to do some of the work."

"Bill is so good-hearted," Deedee whispered to Margaret.

"And that's not all, folks. I've brought four fantastic steaks, and tonight I'll show you how to grill good beef."

"Indeed! Well, well!" said Cornelius, abashed and searching for a change of subject. "By the way, do you people like old cemeteries? There's an abandoned graveyard back in the woods that's rich in history. The tombstones," he explained, picking up speed, "bear the names of old lumberjacks. At one time this was the finest lumbering country in the Midwest. There were fifty sawmills in the vicinity, and fifty saloons."

Cornelius was launching his favorite subject, on which he had done considerable research.

He told how—when the log drive came down the river in the spring—thousands of loggers, wearing beards and red sashes, stormed the sawdust towns, howling and squirting tobacco juice and drinking everything in sight. The steel calks on their boots, sharp as ice picks, splintered the wooden sidewalks. They punctured stomachs, too, when a fight started. Loggers killed in saloon brawls were either dumped in the lake or—if they had any wages left—given burial in the cemetery. Twelve dollars bought a tombstone, inscription included.

"After the lumbering industry moved west," Cornelius went on, "the sawdust towns were destroyed by fire, but the tombstones can still be seen, with epitaphs referring to smallpox and moosebirds. When a lumberjack was killed—or sluiced, as they used to say—he was said to be reincarnated as a moosebird. Smallpox was a term used to describe a man's body when it had been punctured by steel calks."

Margaret said: "We have two favorite stones—with misspelled inscriptions. Morgan Black was 'sloosed' in 1861 and Pigtail Beebe 'died with his corks on' in that same year."

"Let's go!" Bill shouted. "I've got to see that boneyard. I feel like an old moosebird myself."

"Is there any poison ivy?" Deedee asked, shrinking into her chair.

"Absolutely none," Margaret reassured her. "We visit the cemetery every weekend."

Percy was glad to see the party leave for their stroll. They returned all too soon, and it was apparent that the adventure had captured the imagination of Bill Diddleton.

"It's a filthy shame to let that cemetery go to pot," he said. "It would be fun to clear out the weeds, straighten the tombstones, and build a rail fence around it. I'd like to spend a week up here and fix it up." A significant silence ensued, but he was not discouraged. "Hey, do any of those boys ever walk? What I mean, do you ever see any ghosts around here?"

His wife protested. "Bill! Don't even suggest it!"

"I'll bet I could go into a trance and get a couple of spirits to pay us a visit tonight." He winked at Cornelius. "How about if I have a try at Morgan Black and Pigtail Beebe?"

They were sitting around the fireplace after dinner. Bill threw his head back, stiffened his body, rolled his eyes, and started to mumble. An unearthly silence descended on the chalet, except for the snapping of logs in the fireplace.

Margaret shivered, and in a moment Deedee screeched: "Stop it! It's too spooky! It makes me nervous."

Bill jumped up and stirred the fire. "Okay, how about a nightcap? We better hit the sack if we're going fishing at five in the morning. Hey, Meg honey, I'm leaving the Lucky Seven on the bar to ripen overnight. The cat won't get into it, will he?"

"Of course not," Margaret said, and Percy—who had been watching the proceedings with disdain—turned his head away with a shudder.

After the others had retired he prowled around the chalet in the dark, stretching with a sense of relief. The fire had burned down to a dull glow. It was a peaceful moonless night with nothing beyond the chalet windows but black sky, black lake, and black pine trees.

Percy settled down on the hearth rug and was moistly licking his fur in the warmth of the waning fire when a sound in the top of the pines made him pause with his tongue extended. It was like the moaning of the upper branches that gave warning of a storm, yet his whiskers told him this had nothing to do with weather. As he peered at the black windows a presence came through the glass. It came gently

29

and soundlessly. A gust of chilled air reached Percy's damp fur.

The presence that had entered the chalet began to utter a low, painful lament, swirling all the while in a formless mass. Then, as Percy watched with interest, it took shape—a beefy human shape.

Apparitions were nothing new to Percy. As a young cat in England he had once tried to rub his back against some ghostly ankles and had found nothing there. This one was larger and rougher than the silver tabby had ever seen. As it became more clearly defined he observed a figure with a beard and a fuzzy cap, a burly jacket, and breeches stuffed into heavy boots. *Click-click-click* went the boots on the polished wood floor.

"Holy Mackinaw!" said a hollow, reverberating voice. "What kind of a shanty would this be?" The apparition looked in wonder at the luxurious hearth rug, the brass ornaments on the fieldstone chimney breast, the glass-topped coffee table with half-finished jigsaw puzzle.

Percy settled down comfortably to watch, tucking his legs under his body for warmth. A musty dampness pervaded the room. *Click-click-click* again. He turned his head to see another figure materializing behind him. Though dressed in the same rough clothing, it was smaller than the first and beardless, and it had a rope of hair hanging down its back.

"Pigtail Beebe!" roared the first apparition in a harsh voice without substance. It was a sound that only a cat could hear.

"I'm haywire if it ain't Morgan Black!" exclaimed the other in the same kind of thundering whisper. The two loggers stood staring at each other with legs braced wide apart and arms hanging loose. "I got a thirst fit to drain a swamp," Pigtail complained.

"Me, I got a head as big as an ox," said Morgan, groaning and touching his temples.

"Likely we was both oiled up when we got sluiced. How'd you get yours, you orie-eyed ol' coot?"

"A jumped-up brawl in the Red Keg Saloon." Morgan sat down wearily on the pine woodbox, removing his head and resting it on his lap, the better to massage his temples.

Pigtail said with a ghostly chuckle: "They got me on the Sawdust Flats. I'd had me a few drinks of Eagle Sweat and was on the way to Sadie Lou's to get m'teeth fixed, as the sayin' goes, when along come this bandy-legged Blue Noser, and I give him a squirt o' B&L Black right in the eye. 'Fore I knowed it, seven o' them Blue Nosers come at me. When they got through puttin' their boots to m'hide, I had the best case o' smallpox you ever did see. . . . Never *did* get to Sadie Lou's."

"That was in '61," said Morgan's head noiselessly. "Good drive on the river that spring."

"An' I was a catty man on the logs. I could ride a soap bubble to shore, I could."

"Still braggin'."

Pigtail sat down cautiously in Cornelius's deep-cushioned leather chair. "Holy Mackinaw! This shanty is sure-thing candyside!" The logger began to sing, in an eerie whine. "Oh, our logs was piled up mountain high, and our cots was on the snow . . . in that godforsaken countree-e-e of Michigan-eye-o!"

"Pipe down," said Morgan. "My head's aimin' to go off like dynamite."

"You think you're bad off? I got a thirst that'd dry up the Tittabawassee River. I could chaw an ear off the tin-plated fool what called us back! Why couldn't they leave us be?"

Morgan carefully fitted his head back on his shoulders. "It's nigh to daylight. We'll be goin' soon."

"No sense goin' without leavin' a sign," said Pigtail. "I'm feelin' stakey. Yahow!" he yelled in a ghostly facsimile of a logger's howl as he upended the coffee table and pulled the needles out of Margaret's knitting. Percy cringed in horror.

Then the logger began to swagger around the room. *Click-click-click* went his calks, although they left no mark on the polished wood floor. "What's this jigamaree?" he said, as he pushed the seven-layer torte off the bar. It landed on the floorboards with a sickening splash. "Yahow-w-w!" There was a distant echo as a rooster at one of the inland farms announced the break of day.

"Pipe down, you furriner!" Morgan warned, getting up from the woodbox with clenched fists. "You aimin' to split m'head open? If I could get holt o' you, I'd—"

"Hit the gut-hammer!" Pigtail sang out. "It's daylight in the swamp!"

Morgan Black lunged at him, and the two figures blended in a hazy blur.

"Da-a-aylight in the swamp!" was the last fading cry Percy heard as the cock crowed again. The blur was melting around the edges. It wilted and shrank until nothing was left but a puddle on the polished wood floor. Then all was quiet except for the swish of waves on the shore and the first waking peeps of the sand-pipers.

Thankful that the raucous visitors had gone, Percy curled on the hearth rug with one foreleg thrown over his ears and slept. He was waked by a voice bellowing in consternation.

"It's a rotten shame!" Bill Diddleton roared, pacing back and forth in his fishing clothes. "It's a filthy rotten shame!"

"I fail to understand it," Cornelius kept repeating. "He has never been guilty of any mischief of this sort."

"It took me three hours to make that cake—with eighteen eggs and seven kinds of booze!"

The disturbance brought the two women sleepily to the balcony railing.

"Look at my torte!" Bill shouted up at them. "That blasted cat knocked it on the floor."

Margaret groped her way downstairs. "I can't believe Percy would do such a thing. Where is he?" Percy—aghast at Bill's accusation—sensed it might be wise to disappear.

"There he goes!" Bill shouted. "Sneaky devil just ran under the couch."

Then Margaret cried out in shocked surprise. "Look at my knitting! He pulled the needles out! Percy, you are a *bad cat!*"

Percy laid his ears back in hopeless indignation, alone in the dark under the sofa.

"It is quite unlike him," said Cornelius. "I fail to understand what could have prompted such . . . Margaret! My jigsaw puzzle has been swept off the table! That cat must have gone berserk!"

Now Deedee was coming slowly downstairs. "Do you know the floor's all wet? There's a big puddle right in the middle of the room."

"I can guess what *that* is!" said Bill, looking cynical and vindictive.

"Percy!" shouted Margaret and Cornelius in unison. "What—have—you—done?"

Recoiling at the unjust accusation, Percy shrank into his smallest size. He was a fastidious cat who observed the formalities of the litterbox with never a lapse.

Margaret circled the puddle. "Somehow I can't believe that Percy would do such a thing."

"Who else would leave a puddle on the floor?" said Bill with a cutting edge to his voice. "A ghost?"

"Ghosts!" cried Deedee. "I knew it! It was that crazy stunt of yours, Bill!" She peered into an oversize brandy snifter on the bar. "Where's—my—diamond—ring? I put it in this big glass thing when I helped Margaret in the kitchen last night. Oh, Bill, something horrible happened here. I feel all cold and clammy, and I can smell something weird and musty. Let's go home. Please!"

Bill stood there scratching his right ankle with his left foot. "We'd better get back to the city, folks, before she cracks up."

"Let me prepare breakfast," Margaret said. "Then we'll all feel better."

"I don't want breakfast," Deedee wailed in misery. "I just want to go home. I've got some kind of rash on my ankles, and it's driving me nuts!" She displayed some streaks of white blisters.

"That's ivy poisoning, kiddo," Bill said. "I think I've got the same thing."

"It couldn't be," Margaret protested. "We've never seen any poison ivy at the cemetery!"

The Diddletons packed hastily and drove away from Big Pine Lake before the sun had risen above the treetops.

Percy, his pride wounded, refused to leave his refuge under the sofa, even to eat breakfast, and for some time following the weekend of the big puddle he remained cool toward Cornelius and Margaret. Although they quickly forgave him for all the untoward happenings, he found scant comfort in forgiveness for sins he had not committed. The incident was related to a new houseful of guests each weekend, and the blow to Percy's reputation caused him deep suffering.

At the end of the season Deedee's diamond ring was found behind the pine woodbox. The Diddletons paid no more visits to the chalet, however. Nor did Cornelius and Margaret return to the loggers' graves; almost overnight the entire cemetery became choked with poisonous vines.

"Very strange," said Margaret. "We've never before seen any poison ivy there!"

"I fail to understand it," said Cornelius.

The Fluppie
Phenomenon

We first became aware of the Fluppie Phenomenon fifteen years ago. My husband and I had no pets at that time, and innocently we agreed to provide bed and board for a Siamese kitten while my sister in St. Louis traveled abroad for a few weeks. Geraldine assured us that cat-sitting would be an enjoyable experience. She wrote:

"I wouldn't trust Sin-Sin with anyone but

you. She won't be a bit of trouble. Just keep her indoors and be sure she doesn't meet any male cats. She's almost old enough to get ideas, and I don't want her to mate casually. She has an impressive pedigree, and I intend to breed her with discrimination when she comes of age. . . . You will be rewarded with affection and entertainment. Sin-Sin has lovable ways and is a very mechanical cat. . . . What would you like me to bring you from Paris?"

"What's a mechanical cat?" I asked Howard. He was tinkering with the stereo, which had been performing erratically for several weeks.

"When I was a kid it was a windup toy," he said, "but I suppose they're all battery operated now."

"No, Geraldine is referring to her kitten," I said. "Do you object if we cat-sit for a few weeks?"

"Go ahead and do it, if you want to," Howard said, "but don't get me involved. I'm going to stick with this stereo problem till I get it licked. I think it's the amplifier."

My husband made a startling discovery very soon; it was impossible to remain uninvolved with Sin-Sin.

We picked her up at the airport. Inside the ventilated cat-carrier there was an indistinct bit of fur. It stirred. It was alive. We placed the carrier on the back seat of the car.

"Now I can relax," I said. "She made the trip safely."

With Howard at the wheel, looking blissfully uninvolved, we drove away from the airport and were exceeding the speed limit only slightly when we were unnerved by a devilish scream behind us. It was the cry of a wounded sea gull, with the decibel level of an ambulance siren. Howard ran the car off the pavement and halfway into a ditch before realizing that Sin-Sin, who had been lightly tranquilized for the journey, was getting back to normal and introducing herself.

"Perhaps she wants to get out of the carrier," I said, hoping that the demonstration we had just heard was not an example of our new boarder's usual speaking voice. Lifting her out of the carrier I had a twinge of misgiving. Who was this lovely creature entrusted to my care? Her pale fur felt far more precious than my dyed-squirrel jacket. Her brown markings were arranged with a chic that made me look dowdy, and her haughty manner did little to put me at ease. As for her eyes, they were a celestial blue filled with mysteries beyond my comprehension.

Nervously I placed Sin-Sin, whose lithe body had the tension of a steel spring, on an old sweater on the back seat, wondering if a ten-year-old cashmere was good enough to offer her.

On the way home we stopped at a supermarket to buy a supply of catfood and a bag of litter for her commode. Would she be satisfied with a plastic dishpan? Or would she expect something in porcelain or cloisonné?

While shopping we left her on the cashmere sweater with the car doors carefully locked. When we returned with our purchases, however, the car was surrounded by curious strangers, and Sin-Sin was outside—on the hood. One rear window stood wide open!

There she sat like an ancient Egyptian cat idol, stretching her neck and accepting the adulation of the mob, which she evidently assumed was her due. I elbowed through the crowd with my heart beating fast and made a grab for her, but she moved aside in disdain and hopped to the roof of the car. There were giggles and guffaws from the crowd.

"Don't frighten her," I pleaded.

Then Howard scrambled after her, making frantic lunges and muttering under his breath as he tried to match wits with a seven-month-old kitten. The merriment of the onlookers did nothing for his composure, and when he finally got his hands on Sin-Sin, he was far from uninvolved.

We drove away from the supermarket and were busily blaming each other for negligence when a sudden draft alerted us. This time the opposite window was open, and Sin-Sin was craning her neck at the landscape and blinking at the breezes.

I shrieked, and Howard jammed on the brakes. Then the explanation dawned upon us. Power windows! Sin-Sin had accidentally stepped on the push-button! . . . Needless to say, she spent the rest of the trip locked in the carrier, protesting at full volume.

Upon arriving at our house the newcomer sniffed disparagingly at everything, declined her supper served on one of my best plates, vetoed the soft bed prepared for her, and ignored the silly toys we had bought. Every movement she made caused us concern, and Howard watched her with such fascination that he forgot to work on his stereo project.

"We're pestering her too much," he said after a while. "Let's go to a movie and leave her alone. She'll get acquainted with the place in her own way."

We went to the show, but my mind was not on the film. Would Sin-Sin hurt herself? Were there any hidden hazards? Some of the windows were open; could she push through those old screens? Suppose she ate one of the plants and poisoned herself!

It was midnight when we arrived home, and as we drove into our quiet street my anxiety turned to terror. The porches, sidewalks, and lawns were teeming with neighbors. They were tramping about and waving their arms in indignation. They were protesting something. They were protesting a screeching, blasting, thumping performance of hard rock, and it seemed to be coming from our house.

A police car with lights flashing pulled up at our door. "What's the idea?" one officer demanded. "Do you think that's a responsible thing to do?—go out and leave the radio blarin' like that? You look like people who should know better."

The noise coming from Howard's stereo was ear shattering, and he made a dash for the controls while I tried to explain to the police and apologize to the neighbors. "We knew something was wrong with the stereo," I told them. "Sometimes it works, and sometimes it doesn't, but we never anticipated anything like this."

The Fluppie Phenomenon

Poor Sin-Sin! She seemed to be suffering most of all. She was huddled under a bed, obviously displeased with the noisy household into which she had been thrust, but she allowed Howard to draw her out from her hiding place and stroke her fur. Clearly he was proud of his success in comforting the sensitive little animal.

We all felt better the next morning. When we sat down for a leisurely Sunday breakfast, Sin-Sin entertained us by cavorting with some little plaything she had found. (It later proved to be a piece of my typewriter.) She had eaten her breakfast hungrily and was finally accepting her new environment. We beamed with pleasure.

"By the way," Howard said, "if you want that toaster to work, you'd better plug it in."

"That's strange," I said as I pushed the plug into an outlet. "I was sure I connected it."

At that moment we both jumped from our chairs as a solemn voice in the family room loudly announced: "We will all join in singing Hymn Seventy-three," and a church organ thundered the opening chords.

We sprinted for the stereo, and what we saw was difficult to believe. Sin-Sin was pawing the controls.

"Amazing!" I gasped.

"Incredible!" said Howard with awe and delight and a little pride. "She's pretty clever, isn't she?"

That was only the beginning.

Back at the breakfast table we were discussing the smart little kitten when we saw her crouch momentarily, rise effortlessly to the kitchen counter, and disconnect the coffee maker. Clamping her teeth on the plug, she gave it a businesslike yank—then jumped down and walked away, her tail waving with satisfaction.

Geraldine's letter had been quite accurate; Sin-Sin had a remarkable mechanical aptitude. We sincerely hoped this sophisticated young thing would know enough to avoid electrocuting herself.

What she could not do with her claws, she did with her teeth. Her powerful little jaws were like pliers, and she was attracted to anything that was operable: knobs, push buttons, levers, latches, switches. Confronted by any mechanical device, she cocked her head and looked at the challenging contrivance sideways until she figured it out.

The kitchen was her favorite playground—a garden of tempting delights. When she started studying the touchtone telephone on the kitchen counter, we tried hiding it in a drawer, but Sin-Sin discovered that the drawer opened easily on nylon rollers. So we put the phone in a wall cabinet, and there it was safe—as long as we wired the door handles together. This arrangement hardly made for convenience, but I shudder to contemplate our long-distance bill if we had not taken precautions.

"It's only for a few weeks," Howard reminded me.

In the weeks that followed, Sin-Sin disconnected all the lamps daily and the refrigerator occasionally. One afternoon while left alone she discovered the electric coffee grinder. She ground up all the coffee beans in the hopper and burned out the motor.

Push buttons marked OFF had no allure for her, it seemed; the ON buttons activated little red or green lights and produced the buzzing and whirring and growling that made her efforts worthwhile. She particularly enjoyed turning on one or more television sets in the middle of the night, filling darkened rooms with noise and flickering light.

In our open-plan ranch house with no basement it was difficult to lock this industrious animal in or out of any area, but bathrooms were definitely off-limits after the hands on the water meter started spinning like pinwheels. Sin-Sin liked to bump the faucets and watch the swirling water in the washbowl, and she could sit for hours on the toilet tank, content-edly flushing. Scolding was useless; the little charmer merely blinked her angelic blue eyes until I melted and gave her a hug.

In time we learned to forestall her mischief, hiding small appliances, camouflaging large ones with rugs or blankets, and devising cat-proof expedients with wire or duct tape. Howard had not touched his stereo for weeks!

"Let's get a cat of our own when Sin-Sin goes home," he said, after she had untied his shoelaces for the fortieth time.

As her visit drew to a close, we congratu-lated ourselves. We had kept her from meeting other cats or committing suicide or burning down the house.

Sin-Sin had one more surprise in store for us, however. Two days before my sister was due to return from Europe, Sin-Sin came of age. She announced the delicate situation at the top of her voice. Her wailing and howling verged on hysteria and continued nonstop for hours. Even though we kept the windows closed, her vocal exercises penetrated the walls, and the reaction around the neighborhood ranged from simple fury to threats of lawsuits.

In desperation we telephoned a veterinarian at his home in the late evening. He said: "That is characteristic of Siamese queens. You'd better mate her or she'll drive you crazy."

"I can't," I explained. "My sister in St. Louis has plans for breeding her."

"Then put cotton in your ears, and bring the cat to the clinic in the morning. I'll give her a tranquilizer."

Howard and I took a couple of pills ourselves. Then we locked Sin-Sin in the utility room, after wiring the laundry faucets and disconnecting the washer and dryer.

The utility room was farthest from the bedroom, but it was not far enough, and the pill was not effective enough to counteract the bedlam that waked me a few hours after midnight. It was worse than Sin-Sin's howling. It was a cacophony of screaming, growling, snarling— like the sound effects from a horror film. I half fell out of bed and groped my way to the utility room, at the same time shouting to wake Howard. As I opened the door, showers of sparks swirled around me. Red sparks and white sparks were shooting about in the dark like fireworks, amid a bedlam of crashing and clattering. While I stood there in dumb panic, the sparks stopped churning and hovered in space. And then I realized that the little red lights and the little white lights were arranged in pairs, like eyes.

Howard stumbled sleepily into the room and found the light switch. The sparks disappeared, and the room was full of cats—cats on the washer, cats on the dryer, cats in the laundry tubs, and one hanging from the circuit breaker box. They were inside, underneath, and on top of the wall cabinets. Gray cats, black cats, orange cats, striped cats, spotted cats glared at us in indignation.

In the middle of the assemblage was Sin-Sin, looking bewildered but proud. By opening the milk chute she had admitted the entire tomcat population of the neighborhood.

We shipped Sin-Sin back to St. Louis with an explanation that was not well received by Geraldine, and eventually my ungrateful sister shipped us all four of Sin-Sin's mismatched offspring.

All four kittens were remarkably adept at operating mechanical devices—not as advanced as their mother, but far superior to the barn cats and lap cats of an earlier era. Furthermore, each succeeding generation has exhibited increased capabilities. Can this technological sophistication be attributed to watching television instead of mouseholes? Or is it the result of nutritional improvements in catfood? It is a trend worth watching, and we are in a position to monitor it closely.

Howard and I now operate a halfway house for wayward or unwanted cats, as well as a boarding school for the truly gifted and a placement bureau for upwardly mobile felines (Fluppies).

The Fluppie Phenomenon should not be taken lightly. The time may come when all household appliances, particularly computers, are required to be catproof. Today's catly mischief could be tomorrow's CATastrophe.

The Hero of Drummond Street

After the unpleasant accident on the Jamisons' front lawn, the cat retired to the shade of a juniper to ponder the situation, and little Vernon Jamison ran indoors and cried for hours. In time his weeping became dry and unconvincing, but still he raised his voice in a penetrating six-year-old's wail. Meanwhile, the neighborhood children stood in front of the house and chattered and shrieked and ogled the spot on the lawn—now covered with a bushel basket—where the accident had occurred.

Mrs. Jamison finally telephoned her husband at the advertising agency where he worked. "Vernon has been crying all afternoon and won't stop," she told him. "I don't know what to do."

"What started it?"

"He pulled the tail off the Drooler."

"He pulled the *what* off the *what?*"

"The tail! Off the Drooler!" said Mrs. Jamison, raising her voice. "It's that gray-and-white cat that hangs around the neighborhood. All the kids tease the poor thing, and Vernon was pulling his tail this afternoon. A piece of the tail came off in his hand, and he's been crying ever since. Now he's running a temperature."

There was a pause on the line. "Hmmm," said her husband. "How's the cat's temperature?"

"Oh, the Drooler seems to be okay. He's just sitting under the junipers with three-quarters of a tail, but all the kids on the block are trampling on your lawn."

"My lawn!" Mr. Jamison shouted into the phone. "I'll be right there!"

Drummond Street, where the Jamisons lived, was lined with split-level houses, all of them identical except for the quality of their lawns. Some looked like cow pasture, some like country club fairways. Only Mr. Jamison's grass resembled green velvet.

Each family owned two cars, three bicycles, a tricycle, a baby stroller, a power mower, and an electric lawn edger, but no one claimed to own the Drooler. He was a large gray-and-white cat with an unattractive habit of driveling. Festoons of saliva continually draped his whiskers and chin, glistened on his breast, and collected in puddles on every doorstep where he elected to doze in the sun. If any resident of Drummond Street sat down in a patio chair and quickly stood up again, it meant that the Drooler had been there, napping and salivating copiously. He played no favorites but gave every household, one after the other, his damp blessing.

The Drooler had another defect that impaired his prestige. Two years before, a TV repairman had backed his truck over the Drooler's tail, which afterward drooped forlornly and was apparently insensible to pain.

The children rode their trikes over the tip of his tail to prove that it was totally numb, and because of his unappetizing appearance they jeered at him and made faces intended to scare him to death.

None of this ill-treatment bothered the Drooler, who continued to loiter wherever the youngsters gathered, waiting hopefully for their insults and purring at their abuse.

"Get outa here, Drooler," they would yell. "You're a sloppy old cat," and the Drooler would rub against their ankles and gaze at them with devotion.

When the Drooler lost the tip of his tail, he took it calmly, but Vernon—who was left holding the grisly souvenir—gave vent to mixed horror and guilt with a marathon of weeping. Only the reassurance that his father was coming home from the office succeeded in quieting him.

When Mr. Jamison arrived, he chased the wide-eyed, thumb-sucking spectators from his prize lawn, then called to his wife: "What's this bushel basket doing on my grass?"

"That's covering the Drooler's tail," she said. "I didn't want to touch it. Vernon is in his bedroom, drinking cocoa."

At the sight of his father, Vernon opened his

mouth in a piercing wail and clung to his parent with renewed anguish.

"Now that's enough, young man!" said Mr. Jamison, removing Vernon's sticky hands from the sleeve of his seersucker coat. "Crying won't fix the cat's tail. It was an accident, and there's nothing you can do about it—except to apologize and promise to be nice to the poor fellow in the future. He's one of God's creatures, and we must treat him with respect."

"He's crummy," said Vernon, sniffling and rubbing his nose. "He slobbers all the time."

"He probably has an allergy. Now make up your mind to be kind to him, and he'll forgive you. Blow your nose."

"What'll we do with the tail?" Vernon whined, clawing his father's coat sleeve.

"We'll dig a hole in the backyard and bury it with a dignified ceremony. And don't yank my sleeve! How often have I told you to keep your hands off people's clothing?"

The interment of the Drooler's tail was observed by hordes of preschool mourners, and the cat himself made his moist presence felt as he rubbed against any ankle that would permit it. The accident that had shortened his tail had not curtailed his affection for his tormentors.

By the end of the week Drummond Street

had forgotten about the tail; there was excitement of another sort. A new row of split-level houses was being added to the subdivision, and trucks and backhoes were swarming over the site.

One afternoon when all residents under ten years of age were supervising the sewer excavations, Vernon rushed home for his third chocolate-chip cookie and said to his mother: "The Drooler's smelling at our grass in the front. I think he found an animal down a hole."

"Oh, heavens! I hope the moles aren't burrowing in your father's lawn," Mrs. Jamison said. "He'll have a fit."

An hour later Vernon raced home for a can of pop. "Hey, Mom, the Drooler's still smelling around. Gimme something to poke down the hole."

"Don't you dare touch your father's lawn. I'll go out and look at it."

The Drooler, Mrs. Jamison agreed, was performing a strange ritual, sniffing the grass eagerly, then retreating and twitching his nose. In a few seconds he was back at the same spot, repeating the performance with evident distaste, sneezing and baring his teeth.

Vernon shooed the cat away, and Mrs. Jamison examined a crack in the soil. "Why it's gas!

I smell gas!" she cried. "I'll phone your father. Keep everyone away from it, Vernon. If it's a gas leak, there could be an explosion!"

Vernon ran back to the crowd around the backhoes. "Hey, I found a gas leak!" he said. "The whole street's gonna blow up. My mother's calling the cops."

Within a matter of minutes two emergency trucks rumbled into Drummond Street, and a service crew descended on the Jamisons' front lawn with testing apparatus and excavating equipment. Two men hurried from house to house, shutting off the gas lines.

Vernon, bounding with excitement, followed one of the men on his rounds. "Hey, I'm the one that found the gas leak," he shouted, as he clung to the man's jacket.

"You're a hero," the man said, smiling stiffly and shaking free of Vernon's clutch. "You probably saved the whole neighborhood from some bad trouble."

"I'm a hero!" Vernon proclaimed some minutes later when his father came home.

Mr. Jamison only groaned. "They've wrecked my lawn! There won't be two blades of grass left."

"I had a cake in the oven, and it's ruined," his wife complained as she paced the floor, trying to quiet the baby, whose feeding was overdue.

The doorbell rang, and there on the front step stood a young woman with a tape recorder. Behind her was a man with a camera.

"We're from the *Daily Times,*" she said. "I understand your little boy saved the neighborhood from a disaster."

"Hey, that's me!" yelled Vernon. "I'm a hero!" and he grabbed the reporter's wrist.

"Vernon!" his father snapped. "Keep your hands off the lady."

"We'd like to take his picture," she said.

"I don't think I want my son's picture in the paper," Mr. Jamison said. "He would be—"

"Yeh yeh yeh, I want my picture in the paper," Vernon squealed. He tugged at the camera. "Take my picture!"

"Down, Junior," said the photographer.

"Honey," Mrs. Jamison whispered to her husband, "let them take his picture. It won't do any harm." So the entire family trooped to the hill of earth that had once been a lawn, Vernon clinging to the photographer's arm and Mrs. Jamison jiggling the fretful baby and talking to the woman from the newspaper.

"Exactly how did it happen?" the reporter asked.

"Well," said Mrs. Jamison, "Vernon came running in and said the Drooler was sniffing at our front lawn."

"*Who* was sniffing?"

"The Drooler. He's just a cat that hangs around. . . . See! There he is under the junipers. He's a mess, but he loves the children."

"He's got a tail like a sheep."

"That's a weird story," said Vernon's mother, rolling her eyes. "A couple of weeks ago my son pulled the cat's tail off."

"Really? Do they come off easily?"

"The Drooler's did. He didn't seem to mind."

"And what happened today?"

"Well, the Drooler was sniffing a crack in the ground, so I investigated and smelled gas—that's all."

The photographer, meanwhile, had pried Vernon loose from his camera and was posing the boy in front of the junipers. "Now stoop down," he said, "as if you were examining the place where you smelled gas."

"Wait a minute," said Mrs. Jamison. "Let me comb his hair and put him in a clean shirt. It won't take a second."

The photographer drew an impatient breath and looked up at the sky, and the reporter told him in a low voice: "It wasn't the kid who found the leak. It was the cat."

"That's even better. Let's shoot the cat." He aimed the camera at the Drooler and clicked off a whole roll of film.

When Vernon reappeared with damp hair and clean shirt, the photographer said: "Now stand where I told you and hold your cat so he's facing the camera."

"He's not my cat!" shouted Vernon. "I don't want my picture taken with that sloppy old Drooler."

"Sure you do," said the man. "He's a celebrity. He smelled gas and saved the whole neighborhood."

"No, he didn't!" Vernon screamed, pounding the photographer in the ribs. "*I saved the neighborhood!* Get outa here, Drooler!" and he pitched a pebble at the cat, who blinked with pleasure and purred loudly.

"Vernon!" Mr. Jamison said sharply. "Do what the man says, or go in the house."

"That's all right," said the photographer, suddenly agreeable. "Let him have his own way," and he aimed his camera at Vernon and clicked the shutter—without, however, putting a new roll of film in the camera. To the reporter he added under his breath: "Let's get out of here. I can't stand a kid pawing me and grabbing my camera. Let's see the TV crew cope with the brat. Here comes their van."

So it was the Drooler's picture that appeared on the six o'clock news and in the *Daily Times* on the following morning. The story read: "A suburban cat with three-quarters of a tail averted an explosion yesterday when he sniffed out a break in a gas main, caused by sewer excavations nearby."

The photograph, which appeared on page one, was a good likeness of the Drooler, wet-chinned and congenial, and both the wire services and the national networks picked up the story. Almost overnight the Drooler became the media cat of the moment.

He is now receiving so much attention and so many offers that Mr. Jamison is acting as his personal manager. Since no family can lay undisputed claim to the Drooler, he has been incorporated, all shares being held equally by residents of Drummond Street. At the first shareholders' meeting a proposal to change the name of the street was hotly debated before being tabled.

Vernon has been sent away to school, and the Drooler is now occupying his room. He no longer drivels. After two visits to the veterinary clinic and a new diet of nutritionally balanced catfood, he has lost his unattractive habit. Nevertheless, T-shirts and bumper stickers still proclaim him as the Drooler, and his story will soon be made into a major motion picture. Meanwhile, news has been leaked to the press that the Hero of Drummond Street will be pictured on the cover of a national magazine, nude.

The Mad Museum Mouser

A police car was cruising down the street as I parked at the gate of the Lockmaster Museum, and the officer at the wheel appeared to be scrutinizing my license plate. It was the first hint that something unusual was happening in that sleepy town. Security is the first consideration in museum management, but small communities rarely provide such noticeable police protection.

I removed my sunglasses, fixed my lipstick, found the Historical Society brochure in the glove compartment, and retrieved the little black box from under the seat. In doing research for my book, *Minor Museums of Northeast Central United States*, I have found a tape recorder more convenient than a notebook for collecting information.

The police cruiser made a second appearance as I slung the recorder strap over my shoulder, scanned the brochure, and recited the basic facts on the place I was about to visit:

"Lockmaster Museum, built in 1850 by Frederick Lockmaster, wealthy lumberman, shipbuilder, and railroad promoter. Victorian mansion with original furnishings. In family for five generations. Donated to the Historical Society for use as museum."

Then I walked up the curving brick sidewalk to the house, dictating as I went: "Three-story frame construction with turrets, gables, balconies, bay windows, and verandahs. Set in spacious grounds surrounded by ornamental iron fence."

The museum was open to the public only in the afternoon, but I had arranged for private admittance at 11:00 a.m. A tasteful sign on the door said CLOSED, but I rang the bell. While waiting I noted: "Magnificent carved entrance doors with stained glass fanlight and etched glass sidelights."

There was no answer from within. I rang again and waited, turning to admire the landscaping. The police car was circling the block slowly for the third time.

The Lockmaster was the fifteenth small-town museum I had researched, and I knew what to expect. The interior would be embalmed in a solemn hush. The staff would consist of two genteel ladies over seventy-five who would say, "Please sign the guestbook," when I arrived and, "Thank you for coming," when I left, meanwhile conversing in whispers about the latest local funeral.

Such was not the case at the Lockmaster, however. As I was about to ring for the third time I heard the *click* of a lock being turned and the *clank* of a heavy bolt being drawn. Then the door was opened cautiously by a wild-eyed and fragile little woman with wispy white hair. She appeared flustered and kept one hand behind her back, while the other grasped a knobby stick, midway between a cane and a club. She was accompanied by an overfed animal with bristling orange fur and a hostile glint in its squinting yellow eyes.

I identified myself, at the same time turning on the tape recorder. The cat—if that's what it was—replied with a deep rumbling growl that ended in an explosive snarl.

"Marmalade! Stop it!" gasped the little woman, breathless from some recent exertion. "Please come in," she said to me. "This is Marmalade, our resident mouser. He is usually quite friendly, but he has had a traumatic experience of some mysterious kind. I hope you will forgive him."

As I stepped into the large formal entrance hall the orange cat arched his back and fluffed his tail, swelling to twice his size, then bared his long yellow fangs and flattened his ears to attack position.

"Has this cat been watching horror films?" I asked.

"Go away, Marmalade. You are not needed." The woman nudged him with the stick, which he grabbed in his teeth. "Nice kitty, nice kitty," she said as she wrestled with him for possession of the shillelagh. I noticed that her left hand was wrapped in a blood-stained handkerchief.

"What happened to you?" I asked in surprise.

"I do hope you didn't wait long," she said,

still breathing heavily. "I didn't hear the bell. My hearing aid seems to be out of order. I think the battery is weak. But Marmalade let me know you had arrived. You must pardon us. We're a little disorganized this morning. I'm substituting for Mrs. Sheffield. The ambulance took her away just half an hour ago. I hurried over as fast as I could to let you in."

From the entrance hall I could see the drawing room—huge and lavishly furnished, but with tables and chairs knocked over and broken china on the floor.

"What happened here?" I asked in a louder voice.

"I'm Rhoda Finney. Mrs. Sheffield is the real authority on the collection, but I shall do my best. Let me get rid of this handkerchief. The bleeding seems to have stopped. It's nothing serious." She turned to the cat, who had assumed a bulldog stance and was eyeing both of us with suspicion. "We had a little misunderstanding, didn't we, kitty?"

He started licking his claws. I looked at him with speculation, and he took time out to hiss in a nasty way before resuming his chore.

"I'm afraid the drawing room is a sorry mess," Ms. Finney went on, "but we have been told not to touch anything. Mrs. Sheffield dis-

covered it an hour ago and had a heart attack.
Fortunately Mr. Tibbitt arrived and found her.
He's our volunteer custodian. A dear sweet
man. Ninety years old."

"Is this the work of vandals?" I shouted.
Marmalade gave me a mean look, and Ms.
Finney continued as if I had not said a word.

"To appreciate this house you must understand the five generations of Lockmasters.
Frederick was the founder of the family fortune. Being a lumber baron he used only the
finest hardwoods in the house, and the construction was done by ship's carpenters. Notice
the superb woodwork in the grand staircase."
Her manner became coy. "Frederick was a
handsome bearded man and had mistresses by
the dozen! We're not supposed to mention personal details, but I think it adds to the interest,
don't you? And I know you won't print it. . . .
Now let us step into the drawing room. Be
careful of the broken porcelain."

The walls were hung with oil paintings and
tapestries, while the far end of the room was
dominated by an elaborate organ on a dais,
above which were four portraits. Besides the
bearded Frederick there were a Civil War officer, a dapper Edwardian chap, and a contem-

porary businessman in banker's gray, double-breasted.

"The four generations," my guide explained. "Frederick's son was named Charles. We call him Charles the Connoisseur. After the war, in which he fought heroically, he acquired the old masters you see in this room, and the Gobelin tapestries, and the signed French furniture. Also the rare reed organ. They're all identified in our catalog, which sells for three dollars, but I'll give you a copy. . . . Oh, dear! There's blood all over this *valuable* Aubusson. Do you think the rug cleaners will be able to get it out? Marmalade has been licking his claws all morning. I think it was the taste of human blood that drove him out of his head."

My efforts to interject a question or a comment went ignored as Ms. Finney led the way into the next room.

"Now we come to the third generation," she said. "Theo was a world traveler and big-game hunter. Also a bit of a playboy like his grandfather, but don't print that. Shot himself in India—*not* accidentally, they say. This is the gentlemen's smoking room."

On the tooled leather walls were mounted animal heads of every exotic species, as well as primitive hunting spears. The orange cat was still following us and was now smelling my shoes and making a disagreeable face.

"Kitty, stop that!" my guide scolded. "It's not proper! Go and watch a mousehole. . . . To continue: the fourth generation established the fine library across the hall—thousands of rare books and first editions. Philip the Philanthropist, we named him. He and his charming wife, Margaret, deeded this house to the Historical Society when they disinherited their son. A tragic situation! He was their only child. Dennis the Disappointment, our custodian calls him. Dennis is in prison now, and we all feel more comfortable knowing he's behind bars. Please don't print that, however."

I had given up trying to ask questions and was following the guide dumbly.

She was breathing normally now, and she went on with apparent relish: "Dennis was a student of mine when I was teaching elementary, and I knew he would never amount to anything. His father believed children should attend public school like anyone else, but things got so bad that they had to take him out. Later he was expelled from *three* colleges—not even good ones. He got into *despicable* kinds of trouble. Finally he was arrested in a . . . drug bust, I believe it's called. . . . Marmalade! Leave the visitor alone!"

The cat was getting chummy now, rubbing against my ankles and taking friendly nips at my nylons.

"Dennis broke his mother's heart," Ms. Finney said. "Upstairs you'll see her personal suite, all done in tones of peach. I'll not go with you because my knees rebel at those twenty-two stairs, but you'll find it well worth the climb. Be sure to see the glass cases with Margaret's collection of Fabergé eggs. She also had priceless jewels that had been in the family for four generations. After they were stolen she went into a decline and died shortly after. Be sure to see her bathroom, all done in black onyx. Philip died quite recently in a plane crash in Europe. All very sad."

We had reached the paneled dining room that could seat twenty-four, and my guide was extolling the *boiserie*, when Marmalade suddenly appeared with a dead mouse, which he dropped on my shoe. I shook it off ever so gently to avoid hurting his feelings or throwing him into a rage. He was a very peculiar animal.

"How very sweet!" Ms. Finney exclaimed. "He has brought you a present—to apologize for his rude behavior. Nice kitty!"

At this point there were sounds of activity in the rear of the house, and eventually a lanky old man approached us. He seemed vigorous for his age, but his arms and legs moved in a disjointed way, like a robot's. Although it was summer he wore a dark business suit, rusty with age and dusty around the knees. Without preliminaries he announced in a high-pitched, reedy voice: "The fingerprint people are coming this afternoon, so we can't open the museum—maybe not for several days. It depends how the investigation goes."

Ms. Finney said: "This is Mr. Tibbitt, our beloved custodian. He was my principal when I was teaching elementary. . . . Now that you're here, Mr. T, I'd like to run over to the hospital to see how Mrs. Sheffield is doing."

"She's all right. She's in intensive care," he said in his hooting voice. "But you never know. At her age she could go off like *that.*" He looked at Ms. Finney's left hand. "Better tell them to put something on your scratches, Rhoda. How's Marmalade? Is he feeling better?"

"He's getting less antisocial," I volunteered. "He brought me a mouse a few minutes ago."

"He was mad as a hornet when I got here this morning," Mr. Tibbitt said. "Growling and spitting and pacing the floor like a tiger in a cage. Too bad he can't tell us what happened last night. I've just come from the police station. Gave them what information I could. This town used to have a one-man police force. All he had to do was help the children cross Main Street and drive the heavy tipplers home on Saturday night. Then the tourists started coming up here and we had to buy three police cars."

The garrulous Rhoda Finney departed, leaving me with the garrulous Mr. Tibbitt. Now, I hoped, I could ask questions and receive answers. "Do you think the vandals were vacationers?"

"No, this is one thing we can't blame on the tourists. There's something I didn't mention in front of Rhoda; didn't want to have to call the ambulance again. Did you hear about the three convicts that escaped yesterday?"

I vaguely remembered an item on a radio newscast.

"One of them was a member of the Lockmaster family," Mr. Tibbitt said.

"Dennis the Disappointment?"

"I see Rhoda has been telling family secrets. Yes, they caught the other two in a swamp, but

Dennis is still at large. He won't get far. He's not smart enough."

"Do you think it was Dennis who wrecked the drawing room?"

"No doubt about it. He knew how to get into the house—through the chute where they used to deliver coal in the old days."

"Was it retaliation for being disinherited? Why did he concentrate on the drawing room? Why didn't he just burn the house down?"

"Not smart enough to think of it. The police found a screwdriver on the floor, and they think he intended to mutilate his father's portrait over the organ. He's a sick boy. Whatever he was trying to do, the cat evidently stopped him. Those sharp fangs could tap a vein, you know. The way I figure it, Dennis was creeping into the dark room and stepped on Marmalade's tail, and all of a sudden he's attacked by seven wildcats, all screeching and biting and clawing."

"So your official mouser doubles as a security guard?"

"Well, I have a theory," Mr. Tibbitt said with a glint of excitement in his filmy eyes. "Marmalade spends most of his time watching the back corner of the organ when he isn't sleeping, and I think there's an important mousehole behind it. He always gets perturbed when I plug up one of his mouseholes, but I've never seen him so mad as he was this morning."

"No wonder!" I said. "He thought someone was threatening his prime source of supply."

"Let's try an experiment to test my theory," Mr. Tibbitt said, heading for the drawing room with a brisk but jerky gait.

I followed. The cat was there, watching the organ, with his body bunched up and his head thrust forward. He was the essence of concentration.

"Walk toward the organ," Mr. Tibbitt instructed me, "and let's see how he reacts."

"Are you kidding?" I protested. The retired school principal was not kidding, and reluctantly I moved into the room, slowly and quietly. Marmalade's ears swiveled. He was listening. I moved closer, and he turned his head. Seeing me, he jumped up and glared at me with threatening yellow eyes.

"Keep going," said Mr. Tibbit from his safe post in the entranceway.

The cat's back arched and his tail ballooned and he bared his murderous-looking fangs. This was the animal that had rubbed my ankles affectionately and had brought me a gift! I took one more step, and he turned into a howling, snarling maniac. With a shriek I ran back to safety, knocking over a Meissen plant stand in the process.

"See? I was right," Mr. Tibbitt announced.

"Thanks a lot," I said.

In the weeks following the Lockmaster experience I researched ten more small-town museums throughout the state. What they lacked in old masters, African spears, and Fabergé eggs, they made up in serenity. The attendants said only, "Please sign the book," and "Thank you for coming." There were no belligerent mousers or bloodied rugs.

In each town I perused local newspapers and listened to the obituaries and bowling scores on local radio; there were no follow-up stories on the Lockmaster break-in or the escaped convict. Only the evidence in the little black box convinced me I had not dreamed the entire episode.

At last I started for home, and on the freeway I came to an exit fifty miles from the Lockmaster Museum. I decided to take a detour. Reaching the museum during visiting hours, I found several cars parked at the curb and not a police car in sight. A sign in the door said: OPEN—WALK IN.

The mild-mannered, white-haired attendants

sat at the reception desk, discussing arthritis. "Please sign the guest book," said one of them. "Catalogs are three dollars," said the other.

The drawing room was now in perfect order, and visitors tiptoed through the rooms, speaking in whispers. In vain I looked for Rhoda Finney and Marmalade and Mr. Tibbitt. . . . It *had* been a dream; the little black box lied!

I wandered through the main floor, then climbed the twenty-two stairs to have another look at the black onyx bathroom and the Fabergé eggs. And there—among the peach velvet draperies and peach satin boudoir chairs—I found an old man in a dark business suit, down on his knees, plugging a mousehole. The work was being supervised by a *sleek gray cat!*

"Mr. Tibbitt!" I cried. "Remember me? Where's Marmalade?"

He struggled to his feet, unlocking one joint at a time. "Marmalade took early retirement," he said in the thin high-pitched voice I remembered. "The poor cat went off his rocker completely, harassing visitors and intimidating the volunteer guides. He never got over his bad experience. He lives with me now."

"Does he miss his rich diet of mice?"

"No, no, no. He never ate mice. He was

strictly a professional mouser. The guides always fed him regular catfood."

"And what about Dennis the Disappointment? I haven't heard a thing!"

"He's back in prison, I'm glad to say," said Mr. Tibbitt. "And they found the jewels."

"What jewels?"

"Why, the priceless gems that had been in the family since 1850! It was Dennis who had stolen them. He was living here then, and he hid them in the house, thinking he'd retrieve them when the investigation cooled off. Jewelers all over the world were on the lookout for the stuff, and it was right here in the house all the time. When Dennis escaped, he came back to collect his loot. Of course, he didn't succeed. Never succeeded at anything, that boy."

"Who found the jewels? And how did they know they were on the premises?"

"Let me sit down and rest a minute. I'm getting old," Mr. Tibbitt said, looking for a chair that was not peach satin or velvet. We found a black horsehair bench in the onyx bathroom, and he went on: "The detectives started noticing Marmalade's behavior, and they got suspicious about the organ. They remembered the unsolved case of the stolen jewels."

"But Marmalade was interested in mice, not music."

"Anyway, they brought in an expert on reed organs, and they told him about the screwdriver. The police found a screwdriver near the organ, near the family portraits. Do you remember?"

I remembered.

"Well, that was the clue! This organ expert took the screws out of the wind-chest, raised it a bit, and there they were—diamonds and emeralds worth a fortune!"

I turned off the tape recorder and said goodbye to Mr. Tibbitt. As I walked down the twenty-two stairs he called after me: "Don't say anything about this in your book!"

The Dark One

Only Dakh Won knows the true reason for his action that night on the moonlit path. It is not a cat's nature to be vengeful—or heroic. He merely does what is necessary to secure food, warmth, comfort, peace, and an occasional scratch behind the ears. But Dakh Won is a Siamese, a breed known for its intelligence and loyalty.

"The Dark One" was first published in *Ellery Queen's Mystery Magazine,* July 1966.

He has always been called "the dark one," because his fur is an unusually deep shade of fawn. Between his seal brown ears and his seal brown tail, the silky back shades hardly at all. Only his soft underside is pale. He is a husky cat whose strength ripples under his sleek coat, and his slanted eyes are full of sapphire secrets.

During his early life at the cattery Dakh Won enjoyed food, warmth, comfort, attention, and—most of all—peace. Then one day after he was full-grown, he was handed over to strange arms and exposed for the first time to hostility and conflict.

Before he was placed in a basket and carried away, a gentle and familiar voice said: "Dakh Won is very special. I wouldn't sell him to anyone but you, Hilda."

"You know I'll give him a good home, Elizabeth."

"How about your husband? Does he like animals?"

"He prefers dogs, but I'm the one who needs a pet. Jack's away from home most of the time. All his construction jobs seem to be halfway across the state."

"Honestly, Hilda, I don't know how you

stand it in the country. You were so active when you were a city gal."

"It's lonely, but I have my piano. I'd love to give lessons to the farm children in my community."

"Why don't you? It would be good for you."

"Jack doesn't like the idea."

"Why on earth should he object?"

Hilda looked uncomfortable. "Oh, he's funny about some things. . . . I hope Dakh Won likes music. Do cats like music?"

Elizabeth studied the face of her old friend. "Hilda, is everything all right with you and Jack? I'm worried about you."

"Of course everything's all right. . . . Now, I'd better leave if I'm going to catch that bus. I hope the cat won't mind the ride." Dakh Won was sniffing the strange pair of shoes and nibbling the tantalizing shoelaces; he had never seen laces with little tassels. Hilda said: "Isn't that adorable, Elizabeth? He's untying my shoelaces."

"Let me tie them for you."

"Thank you." There was a sigh. "Aren't these shoes horrible? The doctor says I'll never wear pretty shoes again."

"That was a terrible accident, Hilda—in more ways than one. You're lucky to be alive."

"It wasn't really Jack's fault, you know."

"Yes, you've told me that before. Do you still have pain?"

"Not too much, but I'll always have this ugly limp. That's one reason I don't mind hiding away in the country."

Then Dakh Won was handed over, making a small verbal protest and spreading his toes in apprehension, but when he found himself in a covered basket, he settled down and was quiet throughout the long journey. Occasionally he felt reassured by strong fingers that reached into the basket, and he amiably allowed his ears to be flattened and his fur gently ruffled.

Dakh Won's adopted home was a small house in the country, overlooking a ravine—a fascinating new world of fringed rugs, cozy heat registers, wide windowsills, soft chairs, and a grand piano.

He soon discovered the joys of sitting in this elevated box with half-opened lid, but it proved to be off-limits to cats. After lights were turned out for the night he was welcome, however, to share a soft bed with a warm armpit and reassuring heartbeat. That was where he slept—except on weekends.

"Hilda, I'm telling you for the last time: Get that animal out of this bed!"

"He isn't bothering you, Jack. He's over on my side."

"I don't want him in this bedroom! Lock him up in the basement."

"It's damp down there. He'll howl all night."

"Okay, if that cat's more important than me, I'll go down and bunk on the sofa."

"Don't bother. I'll sleep on the sofa myself."

"Thanks."

"I knew you'd like the idea."

"Don't slam the door."

Dakh Won jumped out of the warm bed and followed the bedroom slippers as they moved slowly down the stairs, one careful step at a time. His ears were laid back, and his fur was sharply ridged. He disliked loud voices, and the tension that he sensed made him vaguely uncomfortable.

Quarreling was not the only discomfort on weekends. There was the onslaught of feet. Nowhere on the floor could Dakh Won feel safe. He liked to sprawl full length in any patch of sun that warmed the rug. The floor was his domain, and feet were expected to detour. But on weekends his rights were ignored.

One Saturday he waked with a snarl of anguish when a crushing weight came down on the tip of his tail, and the next day he received a cruel blow to his soft underside when he was stretched trustingly in the middle of the hallway.

"Damn that cat! I tripped over him! I could have broke my leg. *Hilda, do you hear me?*"

"You should look where you're going. Have you been drinking again?"

"You think more of that stinking beast than you do of me."

"He smells better than that cigar you're smoking."

"It's my house, and I'll smoke what I like and walk where I like, and if that flea bait don't keep out of my way—"

"You're beginning to talk like those trashy people you associate with."

"If he don't keep out of my way, I'll drown him!"

"He doesn't have fleas, and you're not going to touch him. He's mine. I'm not going to die of loneliness in this godforsaken place. You don't know what it's like to be isolated all week—"

"What's wrong with you women? You want all kinds of labor-saving gadgets, and then you gripe about having nothing to do. Why don't you bake some bread or something instead of buying everything ready-made, if you're so bored?"

"Stop pacing up and down—or else take those clumsy boots off. You're ruining the floor."

"Try scrubbing clothes with a washboard, if you're so bored."

"I'm a pianist, not a laundress. You seem to forget that I gave up a career to marry you. One of these days I'm going to start giving lessons—"

"And let people think I can't support a . . . a sick wife?"

"If you'd stop pacing the floor and listen—"

"And have a lot of dirty farmers' kids tramping through the house? Over my dead body!"

"Look out! You almost stepped on his paw!"

"Fool cat!"

Dakh Won soon learned to keep out of sight on weekends. Most of the time he stayed outdoors. He liked high places, and the path that ran along the edge of the ravine was a balcony overlooking Dakh Won's universe. At the bottom of the rocky slope there was a gurgling stream with woods beyond it and mysterious noises in the underbrush.

Dakh Won could sit on the ravine trail for hours, entertaining his senses. He watched a leaf being tickled by the breeze, smelled wild cherries and the toasted aroma of earth warmed by the sun, tasted bitter grass and the sourness of insects that he caught with his paw, heard the whispers of the soil as a root reached down for moisture.

His ear was also tuned to sounds from the house—the loud and jarring voices, the slamming doors, the stamping of the cruel boots. High-laced, thick-soled, blunt-toed, they made him feel like a small and vulnerable creature.

When the weekend was over, he again felt safe. As if he knew he was needed, he stayed close, sitting on the piano bench while fingers danced on the keys and a foot tapped the pedal. The shoes were tied with leather tassles that bounced with every move.

Afternoons he followed the bobbing tassels down the ravine trail. The path was a narrow aisle of well-trodden clay, bordered on one side by wild cherry bushes and on the other by clumps of grass that drooped over the edge of the ravine. The tassled shoes always walked haltingly down the ravine trail, stopping to rest at a rustic bench before continuing to the wire fence at the end. There was a gate there, and another house beyond, but the tasseled shoes never went farther than the fence.

One day following the afternoon walk, the big round table in the kitchen was set with a single plate and a single cup and saucer, and Dakh Won sat on a chair to watch morsels of food passing from plate to fork to mouth.

"You're good company, Dakh Won. You're my best friend."

He squeezed his eyes.

"You're a big, strong, brave, intelligent cat."

Dakh Won licked a paw and passed it modestly over his seal brown mask.

"Would you like a little taste of crabmeat?"

With guttural assent Dakh Won sprang to the tabletop.

"Oh, dear! Cats aren't supposed to jump on the dinner table."

Dakh Won sat primly, keeping a respectable distance from the cream pitcher.

"But it's all right when we're alone—just you and me. We won't tell anyone."

For the rest of the week, meals were companionable events, but when Friday night came, Dakh Won sensed a change in the system.

There was a brown tablecloth with brass candlesticks and two plates instead of one. Alone in the kitchen he surveyed the table setting. The spot he usually occupied was cluttered with dinnerware, but there was plenty of room between the candlesticks. He hopped up lightly, stepped daintily among the china and glassware, and arranged himself as a dusky centerpiece on the brown tablecloth.

At that moment there were ominous sounds outdoors. A car had pulled into the yard, crunching on the gravel, and the heavy boots that Dakh Won feared were stamping on the back porch. He made himself into a small motionless bundle. Bruising boots could not reach him on the table.

The back door opened and banged shut, making a little flapping noise at the impact.

"Hey, Hilda! Hilda! Where the devil are you? What's happened to this door?"

"Here I am. I was upstairs, dressing."

"Why? Who's coming?"

"Nobody. I thought it would be nice to—"

"What the devil have you done to the back door?"

"That's a cat-hatch. I had it installed so Dakh Won can go in and out. It's hinged, you see—"

"A cat-hatch! You've ruined a perfectly good door! Who made it? Who cut the thing?"

"A very nice man from the farm down the road. It didn't cost anything, if that's what you're worried about."

"How did you meet this man? Why didn't it cost anything?"

"Well, I was taking my walk along the ravine—the way the doctor said I should—and the farmer was mending the fence around his property, so we started talking. Dakh Won was with me, and the man said we ought to have a cat-hatch. So he came over with a box of tools—"

"And you had this man in the house when you were alone?"

"Jack, the man is seventy years old. He has thirteen grandchildren. One of his grandsons wants to study piano, and I'm going to teach that boy whether you like it or not."

"How old is he?"

"What does that matter?"

"I want to know what goes on here when I'm away."

"Don't be silly, Jack."

"You're not interested in me, so I figure you've got something else going."

"That's insulting—and crude!"

"You don't appreciate a real man. You should've married one of those long-haired musicians."

"Jack, you make me tired. Are you going to change clothes, or ruin the floor with those stupid boots?"

"That's a laugh. You cut a hole in the door and give me hell for scratching the floor!"

As the voices grew louder, Dakh Won became more and more uncomfortable. He shifted his position nervously.

"Hilda! He's on the table! . . . Scram! Beat it!"

A rough hand swept Dakh Won to the floor, and a ruthless boot thudded into his middle, lifting him into the air.

"Jack! Don't you dare kick that cat!"

"I'm not having no lousy cat on my table!"

Dakh Won scudded through the cat-hatch and across the porch, pausing long enough to lick his quivering body before heading for the ravine. In the weeds alongside the trail he hunched himself into a pensive bundle and listened to the buzzing of evening insects.

Soon he heard the car drive away with more than the usual noise, and then he saw the shoe with bobbing tassels limping down the path.

The Dark One

"Dakh Won! Where are you? . . . Poor cat! Are you hurt?"

Strong hands lifted Dakh Won and smoothed his fur. He let himself be hugged tightly, and he flicked an ear when a drop of moisture fell on it.

"I don't know what to do, Dakh Won. I just don't know what to do. I can't go on like this."

The evil boots stayed away all weekend, and the next, and the next, but strange feet started walking into the house. The visitors came through the gate at the end of the ravine trail, bringing pleasant voices and laughter and small treats for Dakh Won, and they were careful where they walked.

One night, after an evening of music, the visitors went back down the trail, and Dakh Won stretched full length in the middle of the living room rug. Suddenly he raised his head. There was a meancing sound in the darkness outdoors—the familiar rumble of heavy boots on the back porch. They stamped their way uncertainly into the house.

"Jack! . . . So you decided to come back! Where have you been?"

"Whazzit matter?"

"You've been drinking again."

"I been drinkin' an' thinkin' an' drinkin' an'—"

Dakh Won heard something crash in the kitchen.

"You're dead drunk! You can't even sit on a chair."

"I wanna find the cat. Where's Stinker? I wanna drown 'im."

"Jack, you'd better leave."

There was another crash, and Dakh Won streaked through the house—a brown blur passing through the kitchen and out the cat-hatch. Under the back steps he hunched and listened to the anger of the voices.

"I'm warning you, Jack. Don't give me any trouble. Go away from here."

"You tryin' to throw me outa my own house?"

"I'm all through with you. That's final."

"Whaddaya mean?"

"I'm filing for divorce."

"Whoopee! Now I can have some fun."

"You've been having plenty of fun, as you call it. I know all about that camp trailer you live in. I know what goes on when you're away on a job—you and your tramps!"

"Go on—getta divorce. Nobody wants you. Nobody wants a—wants a cripple!"

"You and your drunken driving made me a cripple! And you're going to pay—and pay—and pay."

"You witch!"

"You won't have a dollar left for tramps—not when the court gets through with you!"

"You crippled, ugly witch! I'll smash your fingers!"

"Don't you touch me!"

"I'll kill you—"

"Stop it! . . . *STOP* . . ."

Dakh Won heard the screams and the scuffling feet. Then he saw the tassled shoes limping hurriedly from the house into the night. They headed for the ravine faster than he'd ever seen them go.

Bounding after them he heard sobs and moans as the feet hobbled unevenly along the trail toward the gate. The clay path was white in the moonlight, winding between the dark cherry bushes and the blackness of the ravine.

Back in the house there were crashing noises and a bellowing voice. Then Dakh Won saw the brutal boots staggering across the yard toward the white ribbon of pathway.

Ahead of him, the tassled shoes hurried on in panic, and behind him the boots were coming.

The cat's ears went back, and his sleek tail became a bushy plume. He stopped in the path and arched his back.

Then unaccountably, with a sudden languor, Dakh Won sprawled on the path and lay there, motionless. Where he happened to stretch his dark body there was a streak of shadow across the moonlit path, cast by a wild cherry bush, and in this puddle of darkness Dakh Won was an invisible mound of dark brown fur.

The boots lumbered closer, the voice roaring. "I'll get you, you witch! I'll kill you!"

Dakh Won closed his eyes. The feet bore down, and the boots tumbled over him, plunging deep into his unprotected side. With a snarl of pain he sprang to his feet—just as the evil boots sailed over him and disappeared. There was a rumbling of loose rocks in the ravine and then only the splash of the rushing stream down below as the cat licked his wounded side.

Only Dakh Won knows the true reason for his action that night on the ravine trail. It is not a cat's nature to be vengeful—or heroic—but Dakh Won is a Siamese, and when people talk about the fatal accident in the ravine, his sapphire eyes are full of secrets.

East Side Story

(The following interview with Mrs. P.G.R. was taped at the Country Residence for Women in December 1985, for the Oral History Project of Gattville Community College.)

Yes, of course I shall be happy to give you my recollections of the 1920s. What interests you in particular, my dear?

What was it like to be a woman in the twenties?

Oh, it was glorious! We had recently gained the right to vote, you know. We bobbed our hair and bobbed our skirts up above the knee and burned our petticoats. They called us flappers. My parents were shocked because I danced the wicked Charleston and smoked cigarettes in long holders and tried to look flat chested. Some of us went to Paris and *really* kicked up our heels. Those were the days!

Best of all, we were free to choose glamorous careers—not just schoolteaching and stenography. We felt gloriously *in the swim,* don't you know.

What careers did you consider glamorous?

Advertising . . . journalism . . . merchandising . . . publishing, and so forth. I trained as a commercial artist, and I shall never forget my first job with an advertising agency. It was across the street from Cat Canyon. Do you know about the Palace Theater scandal? No, of course you don't. You are too young.

What was Cat Canyon?

An *enormous* hole in the ground, filled with stray cats! At first the newspapers called it a civic disgrace and a monument to corruption. It all started when they tore down the Palace Theater. But first let me ring for tea. . . . Hello,

Marie? May we have a pot of tea and some cookies brought up to 105? Two teacups, please. I have a guest. Thank you, Marie.

Now what was I about to say? Ah, yes, the Palace Theater. It looked like a Greek temple and had been there *forever* and was famous for its acoustics. All the great names had appeared there—Caruso, Mrs. Barrymore, the divine Sarah—all of those.

Where was it located?

Right downtown, on the East Side. The freeway cuts through there now. In the twenties downtown was exciting and civilized and clean and *safe*. It was a crime to tear down the Palace Theater, but some real estate speculators wanted to build a *huge* twenty-two-story office building.

Didn't anyone try to stop them?

A few persons wrote irate letters to the newspapers, but there were no demonstrations or campaigns such as we have today. Militant demonstrations were reserved for woman suffrage, the labor movement, and Prohibition.

So they tore down the theater and excavated a whole city block on the East Side for the new skyscraper. They had just started constructing the foundation when the city put a stop to the work. Not only was the concrete substandard, but the engineering concept was found to be faulty! Also, one of the principals in the scheme embezzled a lot of money, and there were criminal trials, exposés of political graft, lawsuits, and a suicide. It dragged through the courts and across the front pages of the newspapers for years. Meanwhile, they put a fence around the excavation—and then a strange thing happened. All the wild cats and stray cats of the city discovered that big hole filled with chunks of concrete—just as they discovered the cemeteries in Paris and the ruins in Rome. Have you been to Europe, my dear? You should go while you are young.

What was the public reaction to this invasion?

Why, people started wandering over to the East Side to watch the *scores* of cats cavorting in the excavation, and it became a genuine tourist attraction. That's when one of the local columnists named it Cat Canyon, and the city built a special *viewing fence*.

What is a viewing fence?

This one was just a wooden fence with three horizontal rails, but the top rail was a wide shelf, so sightseers could lean on it comfortably. It was also a handy place to set a lunchbox and thermos, and persons working in the vicinity spent their lunch hours there.

The commercial buildings around the Canyon were four or five stories high, with *no elevators!* There were little hotels, nice restaurants, dress shops, art galleries, millinery shops. No doubt you have never *seen* a millinery shop, my dear, but in those days they were more important than filling stations. We *all* wore hats, but not many of us had automobiles.

The advertising agency was upstairs above an art gallery, overlooking Cat Canyon, and on my first day at work I could hardly *wait* for lunchtime so I could take my sketch pad to the viewing fence.

The excavation was deep but cluttered with concrete posts and slabs and ledges, with weeds growing in the cracks. All kinds of cats were jumping around like mountain goats and chasing each other and nibbling the weeds and washing themselves in the sun.

There was one fluffy white cat who was different. She was young, I could tell, but she didn't frolic with the other kittens. She sat on an elevated ledge in the sun—very calm and aloof, like a princess on a throne.

I was standing at the fence, sketching her,

when a young man walked over and looked at my drawings. "You're very good," he said. "Are you from one of the art galleries?"

"No," I told him. "I've just started to work at the advertising agency. I *adore* this fence. It's such a clever idea."

"Thank you," he said. "My firm designed it. I'm an architect." He was a nice young man, and I thought architects were *terribly* glamorous. He was taking snapshots of the Canyon with one of those little box cameras that sold for a dollar. And for your information, my dear, they took better pictures than some of today's complicated contrivances.

The young man said: "I never get tired of looking at the abstract architecture of this excavation—the planes and angles and massing and elevations and depressions. It's like a miniature medieval city—two cities, really, with a battlefield in between."

He told me how the cats on one side of the hole never mingled with those on the other side, except at night. When the moon was in a certain phase, the two tribes met on the concrete slab in the middle and engaged in *horrendous* battles.

The cats on the other side were rather drab—mostly gray—but on our side there were orange, black, calico, gray-and-white, all kinds of mixtures. The architect—his name was Paul—called them the Grays and the Motleys.

He said: "If you come here often enough, you can figure out who is the king of each principality, and which cats are his warriors. The king of the Motleys is that fierce-looking black-and-white tomcat."

Then I said: "That little white one sitting on a ledge is a princess. She never does anything common—like chasing butterflies or wrestling with the other kittens. She just sits on her throne and thinks beautiful thoughts. Whenever she steps down, she walks slowly in a regal way."

And now, my dear, here comes our tea. . . . Thank you, Marie. . . . I hope the cookies are chocolate-chip. . . . Yes, they are! We didn't have this delicacy in the twenties.

What did the cats do for food?

Food? Oh, they climbed out of the Canyon and begged at the back doors of the restaurants. I'm sure they caught rodents in the alleys and explored garbage pails. And, of course, they shared the lunches of visitors at the viewing fence. I saw cats gobbling doughnuts, grapes, olives, peanut butter sandwiches, hard-cooked eggs—everything anyone would offer them.

Sometimes they made friends with visitors and were taken home. I wanted to adopt the white kitten, but my landlord was a *tyrant,* and he simply would not allow pets. The Princess had *heavenly* blue eyes! I discovered that one day when I took my opera glasses to the fence. When I mentioned it to Paul, he said he liked females with blue eyes. You see, my dear, *my eyes* were a pronounced blue when I was young. They have faded with age, I'm afraid.

What did the cats do in bad weather?

There were nooks and crannies where they could shelter, and in winter the city delivered bales of hay to the Canyon, which provided some protection. They were hardy animals.

But let me tell you about the nurse!

The second time I met Paul at the viewing fence, we were chatting about my favorite movie star. Did you ever hear of Francis X. Bushman? He was called the handsomest man in the world. Well, we were talking about his performance in *Ben Hur,* when a strange character got off the streetcar, carrying two large bags of something. Her clothes were drab and shapeless, and she wore men's sneakers. She looked like a *witch*.

"Here comes the nurse," Paul said. "She comes almost every day."

Although the fence was posted with Keep Out signs, the woman squeezed between the railings and climbed down into the Canyon. Then she started examining the cats. One was limping, and she pulled something out of his paw with tweezers. She did things with eye drops and cotton swabs. If a cat looked listless, she popped a pill down his throat. Finally she approached the Princess and gave her something to eat. I assumed it was a tidbit worthy of royalty, like roast breast of pheasant. Whatever it was, the little white cat devoured it eagerly.

Was the nurse on the city payroll?

No, she was a self-appointed custodian—very professional and unemotional. Also very *mysterious*. Paul said there had been a newspaper story about her, but it didn't reveal much. She lived on a farm near the city limits, and if she found a dead cat in the Canyon, she took it home on the streetcar and buried it. Some persons believed she was an eccentric millionaire; you know how rumors spread. Some said she had been a hospital nurse, accused of a mercy killing. Others *swore* she was a doctor's wife who had shot her husband for infidelity and had served a prison term. We never knew the actual truth.

After the nurse finished treating the Motleys, she crossed the battlefield and did the same for the Grays. Then she climbed out of the hole and circled the fence, holding out a tin can saying: "Pennies for medicine? Pennies for the kitties?" Her voice was surprisingly well modulated.

One day I asked her about the little white cat. Why was she so different? So reserved? So aloof?

The nurse looked surprised. "The white one?" she repeated. "Why, she's blind."

I was stunned. "How did she get here?" I asked.

"Some son-of-a-bootlegger dumped her," the nurse said, and she walked away, shaking the tin can and asking for pennies.

There was something about that poor blind animal that tugged at my heart. I pleaded with the landlord to let me bring her home, but he was *adamant*. At the office my drawing board was in a north window overlooking the Canyon, and whenever I glanced up from my work to rest my eyes, I automatically looked for a ball of white fur contrasted with the gray and green of concrete and weeds.

One day I witnessed a beautiful incident. A young cat from the Grays walked boldly across the battlefield in broad daylight. I knew he was young, because he was lean and muscular—a handsome fellow with perky ears and a definite swagger. He spotted the Princess sitting on a sunny ledge and ventured very close to her. Of course she couldn't see him, but I know she sensed his presence. He stayed for a minute and then bolted back to his own camp as if he had been shot.

I saw Prince Charming come visiting frequently after that, and one day I saw him touch noses with the Princess. It was so romantic and so sad—I wanted to cry.

I imagine I was in a sentimental mood because Paul and I were "going out," as they said in those days, and our friendship had reached the moonstruck stage.

What did people do on dates when you were young?

Oh, Paul and I might have dinner at a nice restaurant—five courses for a dollar! Then go to a jazz club or a motion picture. The movie palaces were very *grand,* but the movies were silent and black-and-white, and the actors looked as if they were powdered with flour. Sometimes Paul would come to my apartment, and I would prepare chicken à la king in a chafing dish. Then we would listen to a symphony concert on the radio—with a *live orchestra!* Radio was quite different then.

Were you and Paul having a relationship?

Not what you young people mean by that term! We were enjoying an old-fashioned *courtship.* Flappers were supposed to be cynical about love, but I was a hopeless romantic.

Now I'm losing the thread of my story. . . .

The gray cat was touching noses with the blind kitten.

Yes, such a poignant gesture! It was early October, and the days were getting cool. The leaves were falling, and I had an ominous feeling that it was the *end of something*. Paul had gone to Chicago on business for a few days, driving his automobile instead of taking the train. I watched him chug away in his Model T, and I felt very lonely.

At the same time it appeared to me that Prince Charming had stopped visiting the Princess. While working at my drawing board I kept glancing out the window, and for several days there was no sign of a meeting between the two. She sat on the concrete ledge, waiting and waiting, and I knew she missed him.

Then one day . . . the Princess herself disappeared! She was not in her accustomed place and nowhere else in sight. My eyes kept straying over to that bleak concrete landscape, searching for that ball of white fluff. She was so *very* white! After work I walked around and around the Canyon, hoping to catch a glimpse of her—somewhere. What could have happened?

The next morning I kept an eye on the Canyon from my office window until the nurse lumbered off the streetcar with her two large carrying bags. Then I *flew* down the stairs and across the street, dodging recklessly through the traffic and signaling her to wait for me.

"You know the little white cat," I cried, all out of breath. The one that's blind. Where is she? I can't find her!"

"Oh, *that* one," the nurse said, nodding. "She's dead. I buried her yesterday."

The tears came to my eyes. "Oh, no, no!" I said. "What happened to her?"

"She ate some of the wrong weeds," the nurse said. "Some of the weeds are poison, and the cats know enough to leave them alone."

"But she couldn't *see* them," I wailed. "She couldn't tell they were poisonous!"

"*She* knew," the nurse said. "She knew what they were. They all know. It's instinct."

I returned to my office and wept—until the art director told me to go home. Later that evening I was still moping around my apartment when the telephone rang. It was Paul! He had arrived home safely; the trip had been a success; he had missed me very much. Then, before I could report my sad news, he related an amazing incident.

On the day he left for Chicago he had been driving for some time when his automobile boiled over. They were *always* boiling over, you know. He stopped to pour water in the radiator, and while he was removing the radiator cap he heard some pitiful crying. He lifted the hood, and a gray cat leaped out and ran into some bushes. Paul searched for a while and couldn't find him, but he was sure it was Prince Charming from the Canyon. He had climbed up under the hood to keep warm when the Model T was parked in front of Paul's office.

But you couldn't be sure, could you? There are lots of gray cats.

Wait till you hear the rest of my story, my dear. . . . The next day Paul and I met at the viewing fence at noon. The nurse was making her rounds. Some of the cats were climbing out of the excavation to beg scraps from lunchboxes. And down below, a gray cat was hobbling across the battlefield.

"There he is!" I shouted. Oh, he was a pathetic sight—skinny and dirty—with one ragged ear, and blood caked on his fur. He walked painfully, stopping every few steps and lifting one sore paw. He was headed for the Motley side of the Canyon.

"He must have walked all the way back downtown!" I said. "Miles and miles! How did he do it? He looks starved, and you can tell he's had some terrible experiences. Has the nurse noticed him? Could she do anything for him?"

Paul said: "I wonder if he burned his feet under the hood of the automobile. . . . Look at him! Where is he going?"

He was looking for the Princess, of course. The battered animal wandered unsteadily toward the ledge where they used to meet. Then he turned away and started climbing up to street level, with great difficulty. I started toward him.

"Don't touch him," Paul said. "He's going over to the alley behind the restaurants. After he gets some food, he'll give himself a bath. A cat's tongue is his best medicine."

As the injured cat limped into the street behind us, I made an announcement: "I'm not coming to the viewing fence anymore," I said. "I'm too sentimental. I get emotionally involved. And I'm going to ask the art director to move my drawing board to another—"

I was interrupted by screeching tires on the pavement behind us, then the cries of pedestrians. We turned to look. Someone was running toward the fence, shouting, "Nurse! Nurse!"

Paul started toward the scene of the accident and abruptly returned. "Come away," he said, leading me in the opposite direction. "Don't look."

That was sixty years ago, and I've never forgotten.

It's a sad story.

Yes, my dear, a very sad story. But there is an epilogue.

I married my young architect, and do you know what he gave me for a wedding present? Two kittens. One was gray, and one was white and fluffy. I named them Romeo and Juliet.

Tipsy and the Board of Health

(The following interview with Mr. C.W. was taped at the Old Sailors' Home in November 1985, for the Oral History Project of Gattville Community College.)

Sure, I'm old enough to remember the Depression. Herbert Hoover, Prohibition, bread lines, soup kitchens, FDR, Repeal. I remember all that. If you wanna know, things was tough then, boy. I washed dishes, did street sweepin'—whatever I could get. Worked on the boats when I could. That was before they tore down the waterfront and built them fancy sky-scrapers with fountains and trees and stuff like that.

What was the waterfront like in the thirties?

On Front Street it was all docks and ware-houses. Behind that was tenements, meat mar-kets, candy stores, a coupla beaneries, two churches, a school. Blind pigs, too, but that was before Repeal. It was a nice neighborhood. Everybody knowed everybody. The school had one of them fire-escape chutes from the second floor. Looked like a big tin sewer pipe. That's all gone now.

Fella come to see me last week. Used to be a butcher at Nick's Market on the waterfront. "Porky" is what we called him. He's still fat as a pig and smokin' them stinko cigars. We talked about the old days. Hamburger, thirteen cents a pound. Trolley cars, a nickel a ride. Porky says to me: "Betcha you don't remember Tipsy and the Board of Health."

I says: "Betcha two bits I do. I told my grandkids about Tipsy. They'll be talkin' about her long after you and me cash in our chips."

What did you tell your grandchildren?

Tipsy and the Board of Health

Tell 'em? How Tipsy made us laugh when there wasn't much to laugh about. No jobs. No unemployment insurance. Couldn't pay the rent. Some folks would starve before they'd go on welfare in them days. That was what the Depression was like, boy. But Tipsy made us laugh.

Who was Tipsy?

Funniest cat you ever laid eyes on! She hung around Nick's Market, huntin' for mice. They didn't have fancy pet foods then, I don't think. Folks had a hard time feedin' themselves. Cats and dogs, they had to rustle up their own grub.

How was Tipsy involved with the Board of Health?

Well, now, that's a tale! I was there when the inspector first seen Tipsy. I went over to Nick's Market to get a chaw on credit and shoot the breeze with Porky. Mrs. Nick was behind the cash register, scowlin' like a bulldog. Nick, he was still in the hoosegow doin' time for bootleggin'. And Tipsy, she was in the front window, smack between the carrots and cabbages, givin' herself a bath. Cleanest thing in the whole store, if you wanna know.

So, in walked this fella in a brown suit and white shirt and tie, lookin' like City Hall. Carried a big thick book with black covers. He stuck his nose in the meat cooler, sniffed in the backroom, and wrote somethin' in his book. He gave Tipsy a sour look, but she gave him no mind—just scratched her ear.

Then the man says to Mrs. Nick: "Two weeks to clean up the store and dispose of the animal."

Mrs. Nick give him a fierce look. "Animal? You tell me *what* about animal?" Her English wasn't so good.

"Get rid of the cat!" the inspector says loud and clear. "The cat! The cat in the window!"

Mrs. Nick stands there with her arms folded, like a reg'lar battle-ax. "I not get rid of no cat."

The man says: "City ordinance, ma'am. No cats allowed in food stores."

Mrs. Nick says: "Hah! The city, it like mice better in food store?"

"Set traps! Set traps!" he says. "If the animal is still here in two weeks, you can expect a ten-dollar fine."

She bangs on the cash register and waves a ten-spot. "I pay now. I keep the cat."

"I don't want your money," he says. "I just told you what the law requires. Get—rid—of—the—cat!"

"I make it twenty," and she waves a tenner in each hand.

So then Porky comes out from behind the meat counter, jabbin' his cigar at Mrs. Nick. She was his mother-in-law. He says to her: "See? What'd I tell you? You gotta dump that smelly cat."

"She smell better than you," she says.

Porky tries to explain to the inspector. "She's from the Old Country. I keep tellin' her you can't have no cat sittin' on the vegetables. It ain't sanitary."

"Hah!" Mrs. Nick says to Porky. "You go make some sanitary hamburger, and this time no cigar butt in it."

Why was she so stubborn?

If you wanna know, Tipsy was good for business. She sat in the window and made passes at flies, but it looked like she was wavin' to people on the sidewalk. The kids, they was tickled pink, and they come in the store to spend their penny. Grown-ups got a laugh out of it, too. It was good to see someone smilin' in the Depression.

Where did Tipsy get her name?

That's the funny part. She was white all over, with a black patch over one ear. Looked like a black hat slippin' down over one eye. Gave her a boozy look. To make it even better, she staggered, sort of, when she walked. Musta been somethin' wrong with her toes.

Was she still there when the inspector returned in two weeks?

Tell you what happened. Porky was always feudin' with his mother-in-law, and he was bound and determined to get rid of the cat. So one night after Mrs. Nick went upstairs to bed, he puts Tipsy in a soup carton and lugs it to a drugstore six blocks away. I was there to get an ice cream cone when Porky walked in. You could get a triple dip for a nickel then. Three flavors only. Chocolate, vanilla, and strawberry.

"Hey, Sam," Porky says to the druggist. "You still got trouble with mice? I found you a good mouser."

"I don't want no cat," Sam says. But Porky dumped Tipsy out of the box anyway, and she staggered around like she was four sheets in the wind. You should hear the customers whoopin' and hollerin'. They said: "You gotta keep her, Sam."

So Tipsy moved in. Made herself right at home. She caught a coupla mice and then bedded down on some clean towels behind the soda fountain.

Sam always played cards with us in the back room at Gus's Bar, and he told us what happened the next day. Tipsy was entertainin' the customers when in walked the man from the Board of Health. He gave Tipsy a long hard look. Seems like he recognized her but wasn't sure.

"Have a root beer," Sam says to him. "Is everything okay?"

"Everything except the cat," says the inspector. "The law prohibits animals in establishments vending food and/or beverages."

Well, Sam wasn't one to fool around with City Hall, so he pitched Tipsy out in the alley.

How did the customers feel about that?

They was disappointed, but—you know what? The little devil staggered right back to Nick's Market—six blocks. When Porky got to work the next day, there was a crowd around the front window—people laughin'—kids jumpin' up and down. Tipsy was on the string beans, wavin' at them.

Next night, Porky put her in an evaporated-milk carton and took her to Gus's place. It was a blind pig before Repeal. After that it was Gus's Timberline Bar. He had it fixed up like a log cabin.

I was helpin' out behind the bar when Porky walked in with the milk carton.

Gus give him a wallop on the back and says to me: "Pour the ol' galoot a shot o' red tea to warm his pipes." He liked to talk logger-talk sometimes.

Gus was a nice old fella, but he looked half-crazy. Gray hair stickin' out every-which-way, nose crooked, no color in his eyes. Used to keep a saloon up north near the lumber camps, and he was a tough cookie. When I got to know Gus he was pretty old, but he could still jump over the bar and bounce a foundry worker or dockhand if they was makin' trouble.

I remember the bar—all made of logs, with a pine slab three inches thick. A beaut! There was a potbellied stove with about fifty feet of stovepipe. And all over the wall there was animal heads—deer, elk, moose. A stuffed raccoon, stuffed weasel—all like that. Gus said he bagged 'em all himself, but nobody believed it. He was soft on animals. We guessed he'd shoot a man before he'd shoot a squirrel. He had a pet chipmunk in the saloon up north, and some drunk bit its head off on a bet. Gus laid him our good—with a peavey handle.

What did Gus think about Tipsy?

He thumped the milk carton and says to Porky: "Whatcha got in the kennebecker?"

"New invention for killin' rats," Porky says.

Gus peeked in the box, and Tipsy sneezed right in his face. The old fella howled like a bridegroom. "She's a dinger, ain't she?" he says.

He put her on the bar, and Tipsy staggered down the pine slab—the whole length. Weavin' between the shot glasses and beer mugs, with that boozy black patch tippin' over one eye, she sure was a funny sight!

I says to Gus: "Want me to cut off her drinks, Boss?"

Well, boy, Tipsy got to be the hit of the whole blame waterfront. She put on a reg'lar comic act in the bar. Give her a cigarette butt and she'd stalk it, grab it, throw it in the air, bat it a couple times, and then sit on it and play dumb, like she didn't know where it was. I poured a lotta shots and pulled a lotta beer when Tipsy was around.

Gus lived upstairs, and he let her sleep on his pillow nights. "The li'l dinger curls round my head like a coonskin cap," he says in a boastin' way, "and if she wants to go out, she bites my nose."

Tipsy went out, all right. She started gettin'

fat and lazy, and we all knowed it was kittens. Ding-swizzled if Gus didn't start buyin' her hamburger and providin' a sandbox so she wouldn't have to go out in the dirty alley.

Did business fall off when Tipsy stopped putting on her act?

Not on your life! Everybody was bettin' how many kittens she'd have and what color. She got big as a barrel, and when she tried to walk you didn't know whether to laugh or cry. Gus was gettin' nervous. He had a box ready for the kittens to be born in, and he wouldn't allow no jokes about how Tipsy looked.

Then one day who should walk into the bar but the health inspector. He sees Tipsy and does a double take. Then he makes his speech about the ten-dollar fine.

After he left I says to Gus: "What'll you do?"

"Hell, I'll just pay the fine," he says. "The li'l dinger is worth it."

Ten smackers! That was more'n a week's wages if you was lucky enough to land a job.

Next night, a rowdy bunch of sailors come into the bar from a cement carrier docked on Front Street. They was makin' dirty remarks about Tipsy, and Gus was gettin' mad. Finally one of them idiots tried to give her a snort of whiskey in an ashtray.

Gus jumped over the bar like a wild man and grabbed the sailor. "You hell-pup!" he yells. "Get outa here before I knock you galley-west!"

The other sailors started swingin' and the reg'lar customers piled in. It was some shindy! Fists flyin', heads crackin', tables knocked over! Somebody musta swung a chair because fifty feet of stovepipe come tumblin' down. Smoke and soot all over the place!

Where was Tipsy during the fight?

That's what I'm gettin' to. The bar cleared out in a hurry, and Gus and me stayed up all night, moppin' up. When we finished, it was daylight, and Tipsy was gone!

Gus was fit to be tied. We hunted in the cellar, the iceboxes, the garbage cans, most every place. I tramped around to all the stores, and Gus prowled around the waterfront. Couldn't find hide or hair.

"She's gone," Gus says, and he blows his nose hard. "The cement boat sailed last night. Them sailors musta stole her. Maybe drowned her." You never seen a man so broke up.

Things was pretty gloomy in the bar that night. The bets, they was all called off, and the place emptied out by ten o'clock. Next night, same thing. Customers bought one beer, maybe, and then vamoosed. Gus had no heart for anythin'.

We was there alone in the bar, just him and me, not even talkin', when we heard a little noise. Golly if it wasn't a meow. Gus jumps up and yells: "It's Tipsy! Where is she? She's trapped someplace!"

We listened hard. Yep, another meow. It come from the black hole in the wall where the stove pipe used to go, and you could see a kind of shadow movin' in the hole. Then a black cat come out with a mouthful of somethin' black, size of a mouse.

"That ain't Tipsy," I says, but when she jumped down and staggered across the floor, it was Tipsy, all right.

How did Gus react?

He went crazy, boy. Yellin' and jiggin' and carryin' on! Word got round the waterfront, and that night the cash register was ringin' like nobody's business.

Tipsy got the kittens all cleaned up—two tigers and four black-and-white—and the whole family was squirmin' around in a box on the bar when . . . guess who walks in!

The health inspector.

Nobody but! Gus took the violation ticket and grinned, sort of. He says: "What'll this cost me, Inspector? Ten plunks?"

"Seventy dollars," the man says. "Ten for each animal on the premises. Payable at City Hall. You can expect a follow-up inspection within a few weeks."

"Seventy holy smackers!" I says to Gus, after. "Y'better drown 'em."

"Nothin' doin'," says Gus. "We'll raffle 'em off and pick up enough plunks to pay the fine."

Well, the raffle tickets sold like hotcakes, but Gus wouldn't let the kittens leave their mother yet. Too young. So the whole caboodle was crawlin' in and out of spittoons when that dog-gone inspector showed up again.

He counted tails and wrote up another seventy-dollar ticket.

"Whaddaya drink, Inspector?" Gus says, with a wink at me. "I'll buy one."

"Sorry. Regulations," the inspector says. He kept shakin' his foot. One of the tigers was tryin' to crawl up his leg.

Well, the little ones got to be seven weeks old—time to pull the winners out of a hat. It was Saturday night, and the place was crowded. Gus was kinda quiet. Looked like he was sorry to see Tipsy lose her brood.

After the raffle he drops a bombshell. He says: "Drinks on the house, folks, till the booze runs out. The city's gonna padlock the joint at midnight."

The customers, they raised a holy row. Nobody believed it.

Gus says: "Funny thing, folks. Durin' Prohibition I ran a speakeasy, and once up north I came close to killin' a fella with a peavey, and nobody give a hoot-n-holler. Now I get me a little cat, and they're liftin' my license."

Porky was there, and he says: "Don't be a dumfool, Gus. It ain't worth it. Get rid of the cat."

"Nope," Gus says. "Tipsy and me'll get a shack up in the north woods, and we'll get along jim-dandy. She'll have a reg'lar hoodang in North Kennebeck. No alleys. No garbage cans. No scummy rats."

And that's the last we ever seen of Gus and Tipsy.

Did you ever hear about them after that?

Can't say we did. But a few years back, me and some buddies went fishin' up north. Drove up in a big RV. Stopped in North Kennebeck to get grub for our camp. No shacks there anymore. No dirt roads. All condominiums and curbstones. Musta been a lotta cats in town because the store had about fifty kinds of catfood in them little cans. I asked around, if anybody every heard of an old fella called Gus. Nobody remembered him. Course, that was maybe forty years before. Time flies, don't it?

We ate some five-dollar sandwiches in a restaurant in North Kennebeck. Made me think back to the Depression—sandwiches for ten cents—big bowl o' soup for a nickel. It was a nice restaurant, though—sort of a log cabin. Folks said it was there a long time. Changed hands once in a while but always kept the same name. It was called Tipsy's Tavern.

A Cat Named Conscience

(The following interview with Miss A.J.T. was taped at the Gattville Senior Care Facility in October 1985, for the Oral History Project of Gattville Community College.)

Don't shout at me! I'm not deaf. I can't see a blessed thing, but I can hear. You want to know how old I am? The newspaper said I'm a hundred, but I don't know about that. The last

131

birthday I remember, I was twenty-nine. Twenty-nine red roses came to the house in a long box. Expensive ones! Most likely a dollar a dozen. They came from Chicago on the train, and the depot boy delivered them on his bicycle. Roses in December! Imagine that! . . . A whole boxcar of flowers came for Mister Freddie's funeral, but that was in April.

Push my wheelchair to the window, so I can feel the sun. . . . There! That's better. You sound like a very young man. Are you from the newspaper?

No, ma'am. I'm from the college.

What? The college? What college? The newspaper took my picture. Are you going to take my picture? . . . Speak up! Everybody mumbles.

No pictures, ma'am. We just want to record your recollections of Gattville in the early days—for the Oral History Project.

Oral what? I don't know anything about that. Are you going to write down what I say? I can tell you a heap of stories. I was a little girl when the granary exploded and burned down half the town. And one summer the circus came to town, and the lion got loose.

What's that noise? I hear something humming.

Just the tape recorder, ma'am.

What? I don't know anything about that. . . . Do you know about the grasshoppers? When they came to Gattville, we could hear them humming before we could see them. A black cloud, they were, over the whole county. Chewed up the crops, trees, everything—even the washing on the line.

Another time, the president came to Gattville. He made a speech from the back of the train. . . . Are you still there?

Yes, ma'am. This is very interesting.

The whole town, almost, went down to the depot and shouted, "Teddy! Teddy!" Biggest crowd I ever saw in Gattville, except for Mister Freddie's funeral. Aunt Ulah went to the depot with a sign on a stick. GIVE WOMEN THE VOTE! On the other side of it said: CLOSE THE SALOONS! Aunt Ulah was a caution, she was.

Where's my cat? I want my cat. Look on the bed. . . . Look on the table. It's not a real cat. They won't let me have a real one, but I like a little furry critter on my lap. I talk to him and stroke him. He's only got one eye, but I don't care. They're only buttons. Could you send me a shoe button? Then somebody could fix his eye.

There were twelve gray pearl buttons on my gray kid shoes. My, they were pretty! I wore them to the funeral and ruined them—walking behind the coffin. It's muddy in April. A cat went to the funeral, too. We had a heap of cats in Gattville. The general store had three. The granary always had seven or eight. Cousin Willie called our town Catville. Aunt Ulah said that wasn't nice, but Uncle Bill laughed like anything.

The bank had a cat, too. They kept boxes of old bank records in the cellar, and one winter the mice got in and messed them up. So they got a cat. Her name was Constance. Black with white feet and green eyes. Oh my! Those eyes! They made folks uncomfortable. Seemed like Constance knew what you were thinking, and she'd look at you reproachful-like. Uncle Bill called her Conscience. He said: "If a burglar tried to rob the bank, Conscience would give him that *look*, and he'd run like the dickens." So then everybody called her Conscience.

Listen! Do you hear blue jays? Reminds me of the funeral. Is there a tree out there? They like oak trees. . . .

Excuse me, ma'am. What was the funeral you mentioned?

Don't shout at me! I'm not deaf. . . . The fu-

neral? Why, it was Mister Freddie's funeral.
Don't you know what happened to him? It was
on the front page of the *County Gazette*.
Everybody worshipped Mister Freddie. He was
handsome as all get-out. Little moustache—
wavy hair—blue eyes. He was just *Freddie*
when he was growing up in Gattville. Then he
got to be manager of the bank—with a private
office and a clerk and a stenographer and all.
So then folks started to call him *Mister* Freddie.
Out of respect, you see. He wasn't old. He was
only forty when he died. . . . Are you still
there?

Yes, ma'am. You're a good storyteller.

The farmers would come into town to ask
for a loan to buy seed, and Mister Freddie
would make them feel real good, like they were
doing the bank a big favor. The women were
always taking him a batch of cookies or a jar
of homemade jelly. He liked gooseberry. The
young girls would go to the bank and get
change for a nickel, just so Mister Freddie
would smile at them.

He was married, but he wasn't happy. When
he was away at college he married a widow.
She was older. Folks in Gattville didn't see
much of her except on Sundays. She was sickly.

Mister Freddie didn't go to church, but

everybody said he was a blessing from heaven. After the granary explosion he organized the volunteer fire brigade. And he got the town to get rid of the wooden sidewalks and put in brick ones. And he got them to put indoor plumbing in the school. When they tore down the old Cousin Johns in the schoolyard, Uncle Bill said they should call the new ones Cousin Freddies. Uncle Bill was a regular cutup.

Listen to that old lady across the hall! She's always hollering. Why do old folks make so much fuss? . . . What was I talking about?

The funeral, ma'am.

The funeral? . . . Oh, yes. Mister Freddie. He was a hard worker—worked six or seven days a week except when he went to Chicago. He had to work late every night because folks pestered him during banking hours. They'd walk into his private office and unload all their troubles. Gattville didn't have a lawyer, but Mister Freddie knew about things like that, and he'd give them advice. Or maybe they were having trouble at home. Or maybe they couldn't sleep nights. Mister Freddie would listen—so sympathetic, he was—and they'd walk out of the bank feeling a heap better. Folks said Mister Freddie did more good than the preacher and the doctor rolled into one. Nobody could understand it when he hanged himself.

Listen! The nurse is coming. I can hear her shoes. They go squinch-squinch-squinch on the floor. *My* shoes never did that.

Time for your pill, you sweet old thing! Hold out your hand. . . . Now pop it in your mouth. Here's a glass of water. . . . I'll be back when it's time for your nap. Be a good girl. Don't flirt with this nice young man.

Hmmph! Did you hear what she called me? I'm not sweet and I'm not old. The silly madame! Squinch-squinch-squinch! I always had nice shoes. I had a pair of white kid with eighteen buttons and embroidery all the way up the side. They were for summer.

Excuse me, ma'am. Did you say Mister Freddie took his own life?

What? Yes, Matt was the one that found him. Matt was the clerk. Mister Freddie always got to the bank early and opened up, but when Matt got there on Saturday morning, the door was locked. That was odd, because it was going to be a busy day—payday at the mills. So Matt went around to the barn in back, to see if Mister Freddie's horse and buggy had come in. And that's when he found him—hanging there! It was terrible!

Matt ran down the middle of Main Street hollering, "Help! Murder!" He ran right to the blacksmith's shop. The smith was the constable, you see. They telegraphed the county courthouse, and the coroner came galloping into town on horseback. He had one of those new automobiles, but he said he didn't trust it. The silly thing was always breaking down.

The telephone operator rang up all the subscribers—there were nineteen telephones in Gattville—and everybody rushed out into the street. Folks couldn't believe Mister Freddie would do such a thing. Nobody did a lick of work all day, seemed like. Except the saloonkeeper. Uncle Bill said the saloon was jampacked.

Old Joshua stayed up all night making a coffin; he was the carpenter. And Miss Tillie—she was the dressmaker—lined it with velvet. Poor Mister Freddie! They laid him out in the bank lobby. They couldn't lay him out at home because of the circumstances.

What were the circumstances?

What? . . . Why, his wife went clean out of her head when they told her what happened. She was always sickly. . . . I want a drink of water. There's a jug on the table. . . . What was I saying?

A Cat Named Conscience

About the funeral . . .

The stationmaster took orders for flowers and telegraphed Chicago. You never saw so many flowers! The whole town went to the funeral. Except Mister Freddie's wife, of course, and the nurse that had to sit with her. The stationmaster couldn't go because of the telegraph and the trains, but everybody else was there— even the men who hung around the saloon and the fat girl from the shack near the railroad tracks. All the women cried. The men got out their handkerchiefs, and there was so much nose blowing, nobody could hear the preacher. Miss Tillie fainted dead away.

Then the men carried the coffin up the hill to the cemetery. I had to walk through deep mud in my new shoes and hold up my skirts all the way. The blue jays were squawking in a big oak tree, scolding something down on the ground. That's when I saw Conscience, the bank cat, walking along with the procession. She was picking her way through the weeds on the side of the road, trying to keep her white feet clean, I guess.

Where are my cough drops? Look on the table. My mouth gets dry when I talk. I talk to my cat mostly. Nobody comes to see me. My mother used to come and bring me chocolates, but she doesn't come anymore.

Did they find out why Mister Freddie committed suicide?

What? Speak up! Don't mumble! . . . The day after the funeral the bank opened again. Matt was dandied up in his Sunday best, looking like a high-muckety-muck. He thought he was going to be manager. I never liked Matt. He wore his hair flat on top. He thought he was such a swell!

They sent a new manager from the main bank. He wore those pinch-nose eyeglasses like the president's, and he had a painful look on his face as if they were hurting him all the time. The customers knew the bank would never be the same. No smiles! No joshing! A black cloud settled over the town, seemed like. Worse than the grasshoppers. And then old Pinchnose started finding out things.

I'm getting old. Where's my shawl? Is it winter? I used to like winter, but it's different now. I never hear sleigh bells anymore.

Excuse me, ma'am. You were talking about the new bank manager. What did he discover?

What? . . . Oh, there was a big hullabaloo! Some of the customers complained they were being charged for services. Mister Freddie had never charged them. Pinch-nose told them only *big* accounts get free services. Well! That started an awful row! They were the biggest accounts in town—the hotel, sawmills, granary, and all like that. Uncle Bill said he knew something was bunco. He did the bookkeeping for the hotel, and they had a big sum on deposit. Pinch-nose said the balance was only half that amount!

Then all kinds of strangers came to town and stayed at the hotel—examiners, inspectors, and I don't know what-all. They found a heap of money missing. First it was $10,000, then $50,000, then $80,000. They said Mister Freddie kept two sets of books. They said the entries were in his handwriting.

Matt told the inspectors he knew Mister Freddie was stealing, and he warned him. But Mister Freddie said: "Never you mind. It will all come out right in the end." Matt was afraid to say any more because Mister Freddie would fire him. That's what he told the inspectors.

Eighty thousand dollars! Uncle Bill said it would take a man a whole lifetime to earn that much.

What had Mister Freddie done with the money?

What? Nobody could figure it out. His

141

widow didn't have it. Mr. Freddie didn't gamble. He wasn't a show-off. Why, he didn't even drive a carriage—just a common buggy. And his sleigh coat was plain wool—not fur lined like the big nobs wore.

Uncle Bill said: "By George, if Freddie was so successful at robbing the bank, why did he put a rope around his neck?" He said: "It's my guess that Conscience walked into his private office and gave him that *look*."

Did they ever find the eighty thousand?

What? . . . That old lady is hollering again. What time is it?

Three o'clock, ma'am. Was the mystery ever solved?

What? . . . I don't know. I'm getting tired. I know Matt up and quit. Went to Chicago or somewhere. Something else happened, too. I don't want to tell it.

It's all right to talk about it, ma'am. It's history.

Well . . . I don't know. . . . Poor Conscience! . . . They found her out in the barn behind the bank. Stiff as a poker! Someone twisted a wire around her neck.

Did Matt do it?

I'm tired. I don't want to talk anymore. I

never told anybody the rest of it. I wish I had some chocolates. Do you have any chocolates?

No, ma'am, but I'll send you some. Won't you tell the rest of the story? You're a good storyteller.

I don't remember. I want my nap.

What kind of chocolates do you like?

Chocolates? . . . I like those little opera creams. Abigail always got opera creams when she went to Chicago.

Who was Abigail?

She got heaps of things in Chicago: silk waists, kid gloves, fancy high-buttoned shoes. Folks in Gattville talked about her. She was over twenty-one, and she didn't have a husband. But she didn't care. . . . She was the prettiest girl in town. Everybody said so.

Excuse me, ma'am. Who was Abigail?

Why, she was the stenographer at the bank! She could typewrite and everything. She knew what happened, but it was a secret.

Did she know what happened to the eighty-thousand dollars?

I promised not to tell, but . . . I don't know. She never comes to see me. We were good friends, but she never comes to see me.

Did Abigail get the money?

Abigail? . . . No, Abigail didn't get the

money. . . . *That Matt* got it. He was the bank clerk. Mister Freddie gave it to him.

Why? Can you remember?

Remember? Of course I can remember! Matt threatened to tell everything if Mister Freddie didn't pay him. Just a little bit at first. Matt told Mister Freddie he could fix it so nobody would find out. . . . What time is it? I'm getting tired.

Please, ma'am, what did Matt threaten to tell? It's all right to tell the secret. It happened a long time ago.

I don't know. I don't remember. . . . It was about Chicago. They were *carrying on*, the two of them.

Abigail and Mister Freddie?

Abigail told me. . . . She would go to visit her grandmother. Then she'd skip away and meet Mister Freddie in a hotel. He bought her nice presents. And they did funny things.

What to you mean by "funny things"?

You know! *Funny things!* Abigail told me. . . . She knew it was wrong, but she felt sorry for Mister Freddie. Her mother wasn't nice to him. She was sickly.

Do you mean that Mister Freddie was married to Abigail's mother? Then—he was Abigail's stepfather.

I don't know. You ask too many questions.

What happened to Abigail after the funeral—and after they discovered the bank shortage?

I don't know. She went away. I don't know where she went. She never came to see me. We used to be very good friends. . . . She shouldn't have hurt Conscience. I'm sorry about what she did to Conscience. . . . Go away now. I'm tired. Where's the nurse? . . . I can hear her coming—squinch-squinch . . .

Oh, you naughty girl! You've been talking too much and tiring yourself. We have to put you to bed now. Say goodbye to your visitor, Abby. Wake up and say goodbye. Abigail! Abigail! Wake up!

SuSu and the
8:30 Ghost

When my sister and I returned from vacation and learned that our eccentric neighbor in the wheelchair had been removed to a mental hospital, we were sorry but hardly surprised. He was a strange man, not easy to like, and no one in our apartment building seemed concerned about his departure—except our Siamese cat.

"SuSu and the 8:30 Ghost" was first published in *Ellery Queen's Mystery Magazine*, April 1964.

The friendship between SuSu and Mr. Van was so close it was alarming.

If it had not been for SuSu we would never have made the man's acquaintance, for we were not too friendly with our neighbors. The building was very large and full of odd characters who, we thought, were best ignored. On the other hand, our old apartment had advantages: large rooms, moderate rent, and a thrilling view of the river. There was also a small waterfront park at the foot of the street, and it was there that we first noticed Mr. Van.

One Sunday afternoon my sister Gertrude and I were walking SuSu in the park, which was barely more than a strip of grass alongside an old wharf. Barges and tugs sometimes docked there, and SuSu—wary of these monsters—preferred to stay away from the water's edge. It was one of the last nice days in November. Soon the river would freeze over, icy winds would blow, and the park would be deserted for the winter.

SuSu loved to chew grass, and she was chewing industriously when something diverted her attention and drew her toward the river. Tugging at her leash, she insisted on moving across the grass to the boardwalk, where a middle-aged man sat in a most unusual wheelchair.

It was made almost entirely of cast iron, like the base of an old-fashioned sewing machine, and it was upholstered in worn plush.

With its high back and elaborate ironwork, it looked like a mobile throne, and the man who occupied the regal wheelchair presided with the imperious air of a monarch. It conflicted absurdly with his shabby clothing.

To our surprise this was the attraction that lured SuSu. She chirped at the man, and he leaned over and stroked her fur.

"She recognizes me," he explained to us, speaking with a haughty accent that sounded vaguley Teutonic. "I was-s-s a cat myself in a former existence."

I rolled my eyes at Gertrude, but she accepted the man's statement without blinking.

He was far from attractive, having a sharply pointed chin, ears set too high on his head, and eyes that were mere slits, and when he smiled he was even less appealing. Nevertheless, SuSu found him irresistible. She rubbed against his ankles, and he scratched her in the right places. They made a most unlikely pair—SuSu with her luxurious blond fur, looking fastidious and expensive, and the man in the wheelchair, with his rusty coat and moth-eaten lap robe.

In the course of a fragmentary conversation with Mr. Van we learned that he and the companion who manipulated his wheelchair had just moved into a large apartment on our floor, and I wondered why the two of them needed so many rooms. As for the companion, it was hard to decide whether he was a mute or just unsociable. He was a short thick man with a round knob of a head screwed tight to his shoulders and a flicker of something unpleasant in his eyes. He stood behind the wheelchair in sullen silence.

On the way back to the apartment Gertrude said: "How do you like our new neighbor?"

"I prefer cats before they're reincarnated as people," I said.

"But he's rather interesting," said my sister in the gentle way that she had.

A few evenings later we were having coffee after dinner, and SuSu—having finished her own meal—was washing up in the downglow of a lamp. As we watched her graceful movements, we saw her hesitate with one paw in midair. She held it there and listened. Then a new and different sound came from her throat, like a melodic gurgling. A minute later she was

trotting to our front door with intense purpose.
There she sat, watching and waiting and listening, although we ourselves could hear nothing.

It was a full two minutes before our doorbell
rang. I went to open the door and was somewhat unhappy to see Mr. Van sitting there in
his lordly wheelchair.

SuSu leaped into his lap—an unprecedented
overture for her to make—and after he had
kneaded her ears and scratched her chin, he
smiled a thin-lipped, slit-eyed smile at me and
said: "*Goeden avond.* I was-s-s unpacking
some crates, and I found something I would
like to give you."

With a flourish he handed me a small framed
picture, whereupon I was more or less obliged
to invite him in. He wheeled his ponderous
chair into the apartment with some difficulty,
the rubber tires making deep gouges in the pile
of the carpet.

"How do you manage that heavy chair
alone?" I asked. "It must weigh a ton."

"But it is-s-s a work of art," said Mr. Van,
rubbing appreciative hands over the plush up-
holstery and lacy ironwork and wheels.

Gertrude had jumped up and poured him a
cup of coffee, and he said: "I wish you would
teach that man of mine to make coffee. He

makes the worst *zootje* I have ever tasted. In Holland we like our coffee *sterk* with a little chicory. But that fellow, he is-s-s a *smeerlap*. I would not put up with him for two minutes if I could get around by myself."

SuSu was rubbing her head on the Hollander's vest buttons, and he smiled with pleasure, showing small square teeth.

"Do you have this magnetic attraction for all cats?" I asked with a slight edge to my voice. SuSu was now in raptures because he was twisting the scruff of her neck.

"It is-s-s only natural," he said. "I can read their thoughts, and they read mine of course. Do you know that cats are mind readers? You walk to the refrigerator to get a beer, and the cat she will not budge, but walk to the refrigerator to get out her dinner, and what happens? Before you touch the handle of the door she will come bouncing into the kitchen from anyplace she happens to be. Your thought waves reached her even though she seemed to be asleep."

Gertrude agreed it was probably true.

"Of course it is-s-s true," said Mr. Van, sitting tall. "Everything I say is-s-s true. Cats know more than you suspect. They can not only read your mind, they can plant ideas in your head. And they can sense something that is-s-s about to happen."

My sister said: "You must be right. SuSu knew you were coming here tonight, long before you rang the bell."

"Of course I am right. I am always right," said Mr. Van. "My grandmother in Vlissingen had a tomcat called Zwartje just before she died, and for years after the funeral my grandmother came back to pet the cat. Every night Zwartje stood in front of the chair where Grootmoeder used to sit, and he would stretch and purr although there was-s-s no one there. Every night at half past eight."

After that visit with Mr. Van I referred to him as Grandmother's Ghost, for he too made a habit of appearing at eight-thirty several times a week. (For Gertrude's coffee, I guessed.)

He would say: "I was-s-s feeling lonesome for my little sweetheart," and SuSu would make an extravagant fuss over the man. It pleased me that he never stayed long, although Gertrude usually encouraged him to linger.

The little framed picture he had given us was not exactly to my taste. It was a silhouette of three figures—a man in frock coat and top hat, a woman in hoopskirt and sunbonnet, and a cat carrying his tail like a lance. To satisfy my sister, however, I hung the picture, but only over the kitchen sink.

One evening Gertrude, who is a librarian, came home in great excitement. "There's a signature on that silhouette," she said, "and I looked it up at the library. Augustin Edouart was a famous artist, and our silhouette is over a hundred years old. It might be valuable."

"I doubt it," I said. "We used to cut silhouettes like that in the third grade."

Eventually, at my sister's urging, I took the object to an antique shop, and the dealer said it was a good one, probably worth several hundred dollars.

When Gertrude heard this, she said: "If the dealer quoted hundreds, it's probably worth thousands. I think we should give it back to Mr. Van. The poor man doesn't know what he's giving away."

I agreed he could probably sell it and buy himself a decent wheelchair.

At eight-thirty that evening SuSu began to gurgle and prance.

"Here comes Grandmother's Ghost," I said, and shortly afterward the doorbell rang.

"Mr. Van," I said after Gertrude had poured the coffee, "remember that silhouette you gave us? I've found out it's valuable, and you must take it back."

"Of course it is-s-s valuable," he said. "Would I give it to you if it was-s-s nothing but *rommel?*"

"Do you know something about antiques?"

"My dear Mevrouw, I have a million dollars' worth of antiques in my apartment. Tomorrow evening you ladies must come and see my treasures. I will get rid of that *smeerlap,* and the three of us will enjoy a cup of coffee."

"By the way, what is a *smeerlap?*" I asked.

"It is-s-s not very nice," said Mr. Van. "If somebody called me a *smeerlap,* I would punch him in the nose. . . . Bring my little sweetheart when you come, ladies. She will find some fascinating objects to explore."

Our cat seemed to know what he was saying.

"SuSu will enjoy it," said Gertrude. "She's locked up in this apartment all winter."

"Knit her a sweater and take her to the park in winter," said the Hollander in the commanding tone that always irritated me. "I often bundle up in a blanket and go to the park in the evening. It is-s-s good for insomnia."

"SuSu is not troubled with insomnia," I informed him. "She sleeps twenty hours a day."

Mr. Van looked at me with scorn. "You are

wrong. Cats never sleep. You think they are sleeping, but cats are the most wakeful creatures on earth. That is-s-s one of their secrets."

After he had gone, I said to Gertrude: "I know you like the fellow, but you must admit he's off his rocker."

"He's just a little eccentric."

"If he has a million dollars' worth of antiques, which I doubt, why is he living in this run-down building? And why doesn't he buy a wheelchair that's easier to operate?"

"Because he's a Dutchman, I suppose," was Gertrude's explanation.

"And how about all those ridiculous things he says about cats?"

"I'm beginning to think they're true."

"And who is the fellow who lives with him? Is he a servant, or a nurse, or a keeper, or what? I see him coming and going on the elevator, but he never speaks—not one word. He doesn't even seem to have a name, and Mr. Van treats him like a slave. I'm not sure we should go tomorrow night. The whole situation is too strange."

Nevertheless, we went. The Hollander's apartment was jammed with furniture and bric-a-brac, and he shouted at his companion:

"Move that *rommel* so the ladies can sit down."

Sullenly the fellow removed some paintings and tapestries from the seat of a carved sofa.

"Now get out of here!" Mr. Van shouted at him. "Get yourself a beer," and he threw the man some money with less grace than one would throw a dog a bone.

While SuSu explored the premises we drank our coffee, and then Mr. Van showed us his treasures, propelling his wheelchair through a maze of furniture. He pointed out Chippendale-this and Affleck-that and Newport-something-else. They were treasures to him, but to me they were musty relics of a dead past.

"I am in the antique business," Mr. Van explained. "Before I was-s-s chained to this wheelchair, I had a shop and exhibited at the major shows. Then . . . I was-s-s in a bad auto accident, and now I sell from the apartment. By appointment only."

"Can you do that successfully?" Gertrude asked.

"And why not? The museum people know me, and collectors come here from all over the country. I buy. I sell. And my man Frank does the legwork. He is-s-s the perfect assistant for an antique dealer—strong in the back, weak in the head."

"Where did you find him?"

"On a junk heap. I have taught him enough to be useful to me, but not enough to be useful to himself. A smart arrangement, eh?" Mr. Van winked. "He is-s-s a *smeerlap,* but I am helpless without him. . . . Hoo! Look at my little sweetheart. She has-s-s found a prize!"

SuSu was sniffing at a silver bowl with two handles.

Mr. Van nodded approvingly. "It is a caudle cup made by Jeremiah Dummer of Boston in the late seventeenth century—for a certain lady in Salem. They said she was-s-s a witch. Look at my little sweetheart. She knows!"

I coughed and said: "Yes, indeed. You're lucky to have Frank."

"You think I do not know it?" Mr. Van said in a snappish tone. "That is-s-s why I keep him poor. If I gave him wages, he would get ideas. A *smeerlap* with ideas—there is-s-s nothing worse."

"How long ago was your accident?"

"Five years, and it was-s-s that idiot's fault. He did it! He did this to me!" The man's voice rose to a shout, and his face turned red as he pounded the arms of his wheelchair with his fist. Then SuSu rubbed against his ankles, and he stroked her and began to calm down. "Yes, five years in this miserable chair. We were driving to an antique show in the station wagon. Sixty miles an hour—and he went through a red light and hit a truck. A gravel truck!"

Gertrude put both hands to her face. "How terrible, Mr. Van!"

"I remember packing the wagon for that trip. I was-s-s complaining all the time about sore arches. Hah! What I would give for some sore arches today yet!"

"Wasn't Frank hurt?"

Mr. Van made an impatient gesture. "His-s-s head only. They picked Waterford crystal out of that blockhead for six hours. He has-s-s been *gek* ever since." He tapped his temple.

"Where did you find this unusual wheelchair?" I asked.

"My dear Mevrouw, never ask a dealer where he found something. It was-s-s made for a railroad millionaire in 1872. It has-s-s the original plush. If you must spend your life in a wheelchair, have one that gives some pleasure. And now we come to the purpose of tonight's visit. Ladies, I want you to do something for me."

He wheeled himself to a desk, and Gertrude and I exchanged anxious glances.

"Here in this desk is-s-s a new will I have written, and I need witnesses. I am leaving a few choice items to museums. Everything else is-s-s to be sold and the proceeds used to establish a foundation."

"What about Frank?" asked Gertrude, who is always genuinely concerned about others.

"Bah! Nothing for that *smeerlap!* . . . But before you ladies sign the papers, there is-s-s one thing I must write down. What is-s-s the full name of my little sweetheart?"

We both hesitated, and finally I said: "Her registered name is Superior Suda of Siam."

"Good! I will make it the Superior Suda Foundation. That gives me pleasure. Making a will is-s-s a dismal business, like a wheelchair, so give yourself some pleasure."

"What—ah—will be the purpose of the foundation?" I asked.

Mr. Van blessed us with one of his ambiguous smiles. "It will sponsor research," he said. "I want universities to study the highly developed mental perception of the domestic feline and apply the knowledge to the improvement of the human mind. Ladies, there is-s-s nothing better I could do with my fortune. Man is-s-s

eons behind the smallest fireside grimalkin."
He gave us a canny look, and his eyes nar-
rowed. "I am in a position to know."

We witnessed the man's signature. What else
could we do? A few days later we left on vacation and never saw Mr. Van again.

Gertrude and I always went south for three
weeks in winter, taking SuSu with us. When we
returned, the sorry news about our eccentric
neighbor was thrown at us without ceremony.

We met Frank on the elevator as we were
taking our luggage upstairs, and for the first
time he spoke. That in itself was a shock.

He said simply, without any polite preliminaries: "They took him away."

"What's that? What did you say?" we both
clamored at once.

"They took him away." It was surprising to
find that the voice of this muscular man was
high-pitched and rasping.

"What happened to Mr. Van?" my sister demanded.

"He cracked up. His folks come from Pennsylvania and took him back home. He's in a
nut hospital."

I saw Gertrude wince, and she said: "Is it serious?"

Frank shrugged.

"What will happen to all his antiques?"

"His folks told me to dump the junk."

"But they're valuable things, aren't they?"

"Nah. Junk. He give everybody that guff about museums and all." Frank shrugged again and tapped his head. "He was *gek.*"

In stunned wonderment my sister and I reached our apartment, and I could hardly wait to say it: "I told you your Dutchman was unbalanced."

"Such a pity," she murmured.

"What do you think of the sudden change in Frank? He acts like a free man. It must have been terrible living with that old Scrooge."

"I'll miss Mr. Van," Gertrude said softly. "He was very interesting. SuSu will miss him, too."

But SuSu, we observed later that evening, was not willing to relinquish her friend in the wheelchair as easily as we had done.

We were unpacking the vacation luggage after dinner when SuSu staged her demonstration. She started to gurgle and prance, exactly as she had done all winter whenever Mr. Van was approaching our door. Gertrude and I watched her, waiting for the bell to ring. When SuSu trotted expectantly to the door, we followed. She was behaving in an extraordinary manner. She craned her neck, made weaving motions with her head, rolled over on her back, and stretched luxuriously, all the while purring her heart out; but the doorbell never rang.

Looking at my watch, I said: "It's eight-thirty. SuSu remembers."

"It's quite touching, isn't it?" Gertrude remarked.

That was not the end of SuSu's demonstrations. Almost every night at half past eight she performed the same ritual.

I recalled how SuSu had continued to sleep in the guest room long after we had moved her bed to another place. "Cats hate to give up a habit. But she'll forget Mr. Van's visits after a while."

SuSu did not forget. A few weeks passed. Then we had a foretaste of spring and a sudden thaw. People went without coats prematurely, convertibles cruised with the tops down, and a few hopeful fishermen appeared on the wharf at the foot of our street, although the river was still patched with ice.

On one of these warm evenings we walked SuSu down to the park for her first spring outing, expecting her to go after last year's dried weeds with snapping jaws. Instead, she tugged at her leash, pulling toward the boardwalk. Out of curiosity we let her have her way, and there on the edge of the wharf she staged her weird performance once more—gurgling, arching her back, craning her neck with joy.

"She's doing it again," I said. "I wonder what the reason could be."

Gertrude said, almost in a whisper: "Remember what Mr. Van said about cats and ghosts?"

"Look at that animal! You'd swear she was rubbing against someone's ankles. I wish she'd stop. It makes me uneasy."

"I wonder," said my sister very slowly, "if Mr. Van is really in a mental hospital."

"What do you mean?"

"Or is he—down there?" Gertrude pointed uncertainly over the edge of the wharf. "I think Mr. Van is dead, and SuSu knows."

"That's too fantastic," I said. "*Really,* Gertrude!"

"I think Frank pushed the poor man off the wharf, wheelchair and all—perhaps one dark night when Mr. Van couldn't sleep and insisted on being wheeled to the park."

"You're not serious, Gertrude."

"Can't you see it? . . . A cold night. The riverfront deserted. Mr. Van trussed in his wheelchair with a blanket. Why, that chair would sink like lead! What a terrible thing! That icy water. That poor helpless man."

"I just can't—"

"Now Frank is free, and he has all those antiques, and nobody cares enough to ask questions. He can sell them and be set up for life."

"And he tears up the will," I suggested, succumbing to Gertrude's fantasy.

"Do you know what a Newport blockfront is worth? I've been looking it up in the library. A chest like the one we saw in Mr. Van's apartment was sold for hundreds of thousands at an auction on the East Coast."

"But what about the relatives in Pennsylvania?"

"I'm sure Mr. Van had no relatives—in Pennsylvania or anywhere else."

"Well, what do you propose we should do?" I said in exasperation. "Report it to the manager of the building? Notify the police? Tell them we think the man has been murdered because our cat sees his ghost every night at eight-thirty? We'd look like a couple of middle-aged ladies who are getting a little *gek*."

As a matter of fact, I was beginning to worry about Gertrude's obsession—that is, until I read the morning paper a few days later.

I skimmed through it at the breakfast table, and there—at the bottom of page seven—one small item leaped off the paper at me. Could I believe my eyes?

"Listen to this," I said to my sister. "The body of an unidentified man has been washed up on a downriver island. Police say the body had apparently been held underwater for several weeks by the ice.... About fifty-five years old and crippled.... No one fitting that description has been reported to the Missing Persons Bureau."

For a moment my sister stared at the coffeepot. Then she left the breakfast table and went to the telephone.

"Now all the police have to do," she said with a quiver in her voice, "is to look for an antique wheelchair in the river at the foot of the street. Cast iron. With the original plush." She blinked at the phone several times. "Would you dial?" she asked me. "I can't see the numbers."

Stanley and Spook

When I first met Jane she used to say: "I'd rather have kittens than kids." Ten years later she had one of each: Stanley and Spook, a most unusual pair. She also had a successful engineer for a husband and a lovely house in the Chicago suburbs and a new car every year.

In the interim we had kept in touch, more or less, by means of Christmas cards and vacation postcards. Then one spring I attended a business conference in Chicago and telephoned Jane to say hello.

She was elated! "Linda, you've got to come out here for a visit when you've finished with your meetings. Ed has an engineering job in Saudi Arabia, and I'm here alone with Stanley and Spook. I'd love to have you meet them. And you and I can talk about old times."

She gave me directions: "When you get off the freeway, go four miles north, then take a left at the cider mill until you come to Maplewood Farms. It's a winding road. We're the last house—white with black shutters and an *enormous* maple tree in front. You can't miss it."

Late Friday afternoon I rented a car and drove to the affluent suburbs, recalling that we had once lived contentedly in tents. Now Jane lived in Maplewood Farms, and I had an apartment with a view on New York's Upper East Side.

When Jane and I first met, we were newly married to a pair of young engineers who were building a dam in the northern wilderness. The first summer, we lived in a sprawling "tent city" and thought it a great adventure. After all, we were young and still had rice in our hair. Eventually, cottages were built for the engineers. *Shacks* would be a better description. Jane decorated hers, I remember, with pictures of cats, and for Christmas Ed gave her an amber Persian that she named Maple Sugar. That's when she made her memorable announcement about kittens and kids. All that seemed ages ago.

Arriving at Maplewood Farms I was driving slowly down the winding avenue, admiring the well-landscaped houses, when I noticed a fire truck at the far end. People were grouped on the lawns and the pavement, watching, but there was no sign of anxiety. Actually, everyone seemed quite happy.

I parked and approached two couples who were standing in the middle of the street, sipping cocktails. "What's happening?" I asked.

A woman in a Moroccan caftan smiled and said: "Spook climbed up the big maple and doesn't know how to climb down."

"Third time this month," said a man in an embroidered Mexican shirt. "Up go our taxes! . . . Would you like a drink, honey?"

The other man suggested: "Why don't they cut down the tree?"

"Or put Spook on a leash," the first woman said. Everyone laughed.

The fire truck had extended its ladder high into the branches of the big maple, and I watched as a fireman climbed up and disappeared into the leafy green. A moment or two later, he came back into view, and a cheer went up from the bystanders. He was carrying a six-year-old boy in jeans and a Chicago Cubs sweatshirt.

Jane, waiting at the foot of the ladder, hugged and scolded the child—an adorable little boy with his father's blond hair and his mother's big brown eyes. Then she and I had a tearful, happy reunion.

"I thought Spook was your *cat*," I said.

"No, *Stanley* is the cat," Jane explained. "There he is on the front step. He's dying to meet you."

Stanley was a big, gorgeous feline with thick blond fur and a spotless white bib. He followed us into the house, his plumed tail waving with authority and aplomb.

Jane instructed her son: "Show Aunt Linda to the guest room, and then bring her out to the deck for cocktails."

Spook lugged my overnight case upstairs and showed a great deal of curiosity about its contents when I unpacked. "Are you my aunt?" he wanted to know.

"Not really. But you can call me Aunt Linda. I'd like that."

Then the four of us assembled on the redwood deck overlooking a flawless lawn and a wooded ravine, its edge dotted with clumps of jonquils. Jane and Stanley and I made ourselves comfortable on the cushioned wrought-iron chairs, while Spook—now wearing a camouflage jumpsuit—chose to sit on the Indian grass rug at my feet. He was an affectionate little boy, and his Buster Brown haircut was charming. He leaned against my legs in a possessive way, and when I rumpled his hair he looked up and smiled happily, then licked his fingers and straightened his blond bangs. I thought to myself: He's as vain as his good-looking father.

As we sipped orange juice and vodka, I asked how Spook got his name.

"He's really Ed Junior," Jane said, "but he was born on Halloween, and Ed called him Spook. At school the teacher insists on calling him Edward, but he's Spook to all the neighbors. . . . Linda, you're the perfect image of a successful young woman executive—just like the pictures in the magazines. I envy you."

Spook said: "Are you a lady engineer?"

"No, I'm an industrial electronic supply sales manager."

"Oh," he said, and after a moment added: "Is that hard to do?"

"Not if you like Zener diodes and unijunction transistors."

"Oh," he said, and then he climbed onto my lap.

"Spook dear," his mother admonished, "always ask permission before sitting on laps."

"That's all right," I assured her. "I like little boys."

"He loves to be petted, you know."

"Don't we all? . . . How long will Ed be gone, Jane?"

"Another three weeks."

"Don't you mind his long absences?"

She hesitated. "Yes . . . but it's a good living. It's paying for a housekeeper five days a week and a good college for Spook and some fabulous vacations."

As we talked, the cat listened, turning his head to watch each of us as we spoke. "Stanley looks so intelligent," I remarked.

"He's good company. He's almost human. . . . Linda, you never told me why you and Bill divorced."

"I wanted a career of my own," I said. "I

was tired of being a dam-builder's wife. The construction camp was driving me up the wall, and Bill was drinking heavily. Things were all wrong."

At this point a robin flew into the yard and tugged at a worm, alerting Spook, who jumped from my lap and chased him. The crafty bird took flying hops just lengthy enough to stay beyond the boy's grasp.

"That robin comes every evening during the cocktail hour," Jane said. "He likes to tease Spook, I think. Stanley isn't the slightest bit interested."

"Are you going to have any more children, Jane?"

"We'd like to adopt a girl. After what I went through with Spook, I couldn't face childbirth again. He was born at the camp, you know—a year or two after you left. I didn't have proper prenatal care because I refused to go to that so-called doctor at the camp. Do you remember him?"

I nodded. "His office smelled more of whiskey than antiseptic."

"He made passes at everybody, and I do mean *everybody!*"

"They couldn't get a really good doctor to go up there and live in those conditions."

At that moment a large dog bounded over a fence and headed straight for the boy. Spook had been lying on the lawn, chewing a blade of grass, but he scrambled to his feet and headed for the nearest tree.

"Spook, no more climbing, *please*," his mother called. "Juneau won't hurt you. She just wants to play."

The man in the Mexican shirt came to the fence, calling: "Here, Juneau. Come on home, baby." To us he explained: "She broke her chain again. Sorry."

Precisely as we finished our second drink, Stanley jumped down from his chair with a fifteen-pound *thump* and went to Jane, putting one paw on her knee.

"Stanley's telling me it's time for dinner," she said. "Linda, I'll put the ramekins in the microwave while I'm feeding the cat. Mrs. Phipps fixed chicken divan for us before she left. You might see if you can find the son-and-heir and tell him it's time to wash up."

I wandered around the grounds, noting the professionally perfect flower beds, until I found Spook. He was digging among the jonquils. "What are you doing?" I asked.

"Digging," he said.

"You're getting your jumpsuit all muddy. Come and clean up. It's time for dinner."

He raised his nose and sniffed. "Chicken!" he squealed, and headed for the house, running in joyful circles as he went. A few minutes later he appeared at the dinner table, looking spic and span in chinos and a tiger-striped shirt, with his face and hands scrubbed and his Buster Brown haircut combed to perfection.

We dined at a table on the deck, and Stanley tried to leap onto the redwood railing nearby, but he missed his footing and fell to the floor, landing on his back.

"Honestly, he's the most awkward cat I've ever seen," Jane muttered. "Come on, Stanley. Aunt Linda won't mind if you sit with us at the table." She indicated the fourth chair, and he lumbered up onto the seat, where he sat tall and attentively. She said: "Stanley's mother was Maple Sugar. Do you remember her, Linda? She had a litter of five kittens, but he was the only one who survived. He's a little odd, but isn't he a beaut?"

Spook was picking chunks of chicken out of his ramekin and gobbling them hungrily.

"Don't forget the broccoli, dear," his mother said. "It makes little boys grow big and strong.

Did you tell Aunt Linda you're going to take swimming lessons?"

"I don't want to take swimming lessons," he announced.

"It will be fun, dear. And someday you might be a champion swimmer, just like Daddy before his accident."

"I don't want to take swimming lessons," he repeated, and he scratched his ear vigorously.

"Not at the table, *please,*" his mother corrected him.

To change the touchy subject I asked: "What do you like to do best, Spook?"

"Go to the zoo," he said promptly.

"Do you have any favorite animals?"

"Lions and tigers!" His eyes sparkled.

"That reminds me!" I said. Excusing myself, I ran upstairs for the gifts I had brought: a designer scarf for Jane; a cap for Spook, with a furry tiger head on top. My gift for Stanley—a plastic ball with a bell inside—seemed ridiculously inappropriate for the sedate cat. A videotape of Shakespearean readings might have been more to his taste, I told myself.

After Spook had been put to bed, Jane and I spent the evening chatting in the family room, accompanied—of course—by Stanley. Jane talked about her volunteer work and country club life and Ed's engineering projects around the globe. I talked (boringly perhaps) about thyratrons and ignitrons and linear variable differential transformers. Stanley listened intently, putting in an occasional profound "mew."

I said: "He reminds me of a Supreme Court justice or a distinguished prime minister. How old is he?"

"Same age as Spook. They say a year of a cat's life is equivalent to seven in a human, so he's really forty-two going on forty-nine. He and Spook were born on the same day, and we always have a joint birthday party. I never told you about Spook's birth, did I? It's a miracle that I lived through it. . . . Let's have a nightcap, and then I'll tell you."

She poured sherry and then went on: "Ed intended to have me airlifted to a hospital when my time came, but Spook was three weeks early, and Ed was away—hiring some more construction workers. The doctor was on one of his legendary binges, and I refused to go to the infirmary; it was so crude. The boss's wife and a woman from Personnel were with me, but I was screaming and moaning, and they were frantic. Finally the sheriff brought a midwife from the nearest town, and then I really did scream! All she needed was a broomstick and a tall black hat. At first I thought she was wearing a Halloween mask!"

"Oh, Lord!" I said. "They sent you Cora! Cora Sykes or Sypes or something. She took care of me when I had that terrible swamp fever, and I think she tried to poison me."

"She was an evil woman. She hated everyone connected with the dam."

"It's no wonder she was bitter," I said in Cora's defense. "Her farm was due to be flooded when the dam was completed. She was forcibly removed from the house where she had lived all her life."

Jane looked pensive. "Do you believe in witchcraft, Linda?"

"Not really."

"There was a lot of gossip about that woman after you left the camp. She said—in fact, she boasted—that her ancestors had lived in Salem, Massachusetts. Does that ring a bell? . . . She told several people that she had put a curse on the dam."

"I heard about that."

"It looked to me as if the curse was working. After Ed's horrible accident there was a string of peculiar mishaps and an epidemic of some kind. And I never told you this, Linda, but . . . Spook was born blind."

"Jane! I didn't know that! But he's all right now, isn't he?"

"Yes, he's okay, but it gave us a bad scare for a while."

We talked on and on, until I remembered that I had to catch an early plane in the morning.

After I went to bed I felt uneasy. Maplewood Farms and the dam-building experience were so far removed from my familiar world of tachometer generators and standard interface modules that I longed to return to New York. There was something unsettling, as well, about the boy and the cat. It was a situation I wanted to analyze later, when my perspective would be sharper. At that moment, exhaustion at the end of a busy week was putting me to sleep.

At some unthinkably early hour my slumber was disturbed by a strange sensation. Before opening my eyes I tried to identify it, tried to remember where I was. Not in my New York apartment. Not in a Chicago hotel. I was at Maplewood Farms, and Spook was licking my face!

I jumped to a sitting position.

"Mommy wants to know—eggs or French toast?" he recited carefully.

"Thank you, Spook, but all I want is a roll and coffee. It's too early for anything more."

Frankly, I was glad to say goodbye and head for the airport. The situation at Maplewood Farms was too uncomfortably weird. I dared not think about it while I was driving. After I had boarded the plane and fortified myself with a Bloody Mary, however, I tackled the puzzle of Spook's tree climbing, bird stalking, and face licking. He did everything but purr! Could Jane's inordinate fondness for cats have imprinted her son in some . . . *spooky* way?

Everything added up. I recalled the way the boy had rubbed his head against me when he was pleased, smiling and squeezing his eyes shut. He was afraid of dogs. He was reluctant to swim. At the zoo his preference was for the big cats! He was always licking his fingers to smooth his hair. Then I remembered something else: Like a kitten, he had been born blind! I shuddered involuntarily and ordered another Bloody Mary.

While the boy had so many catly traits, Stanley had none at all. How could one explain the situation? Well . . . they had been born on the same day. They had been born in the same cottage. For both mothers—Jane and Maple Sugar—it had been a difficult birth. And that disagreeable woman—Cora What's-her-name—had been in charge.

Other old friends from the construction camp had told me about Cora's curse on the dam, and although I don't believe such nonsense, I had to admit that the project and all those connected with it had suffered a run of bad luck. My marriage broke up, and Bill became an alcoholic. Jane's vain, handsome, athletic husband lost a leg in a bulldozer rollover. Other men were crushed under falling trees or buried in mudslides. And, ironically, the dam was never completed!

After lives were lost and the environment was desecrated and billions of dollars were spent, the dam was abandoned. They blamed it on political pressure, cost overruns, a new administration in Washington—everything.

Now I began to wonder: Was there some truth in what they said about Cora? When she was brought to the camp to nurse me during my fever, she was always moving her lips soundlessly. Was she muttering incantations under her breath?

Could she have cast some kind of spell on the two newborn creatures? Would it be possible to transpose the personality traits of the boy and the cat? Transpose their souls, so to speak? I know more about thyratrons and ignitrons than about souls, but the notion was tantalizing. At thirty-two thousand feet, it's easy to fantasize.

That was in early June. I wrote my thank-you note to Jane and in August received a postcard from Alaska. She and Ed were showing Spook the icebergs and polar bears, but he was fascinated chiefly by the puffin birds.

Then in December the usual expensive Christmas card arrived, with a brief note enclosed.

Dear Linda . . . Sad news! . . . My dear Stanley was run over by a bakery truck on Halloween. It was delivering a birthday cake for him and Spook. There'll never be another cat like Stanley. I still miss him. . . . Otherwise we are well. Spook is seven now and turning into a real boy. He's stopped ear scratching and people licking and other childish habits that you probably noticed when you were here. He's taking swimming lessons at the clubhouse, and he wants a dog for Christmas.

*I suppose he was just going through a phase.
Love, Jane.*

My speculations were right! The mix-up was conjured by that bitter, hateful woman at the construction camp. And Stanley's death—in some mysterious way—had broken the spell.

A Cat Too Small for His Whiskers

Compared to other country estates in the vicinity, Hopplewood Farm was not extensive. There was just enough acreage to accommodate the needs of Mr. and Mrs. Hopple and their three children—an eight-bedroom house and six-car garage; swimming pool, tennis court, and putting green; a stable with adjoining corral, fenced with half a mile of split rail; a meadow just large enough for Mr. Hopple to land his small plane; and, of course, the necessary servants' quarters, greenhouse, and hangar.

The house was an old stone mill with a giant waterwheel that no longer turned. Its present owners had remodeled the building at great cost and furnished it with American antiques dating back two centuries or more. Twice it had been featured in architectural magazines.

The Hopples, whose ancestors had been early settlers in America, were good-hearted, wholesome people with simple tastes and a love of family and nature. They enjoyed picnics in the meadow and camping trips in their forty-foot recreation vehicle, and they surrounded themselves with animals. Besides the four top Arab mares and the hackney pony, there were registered hunting dogs in a kennel behind the greenhouse, a hutch of Angora rabbits, some Polish chickens that laid odd-colored eggs, and—in the house—four exotic cats that the family called the Gang.

Also, for one brief period there was a cat too small for his whiskers.

The Gang included a pair of chocolate-point Siamese, a tortoiseshell Persian, and a red Abyssinian. Their pedigrees were impressive, and they seemed to know it. They never soiled their feet by going out-of-doors but were quite happy in a spacious suite furnished with plush carpet, cushioned perches, an upholstered ladder, secret hideaways, and four sleeping baskets. Sunny windows overlooked the waterwheel, in which birds now made their nests, and for good weather there was a screened balcony. Four commodes in the bathroom were inscribed with their names.

When the cat who was too small for his whiskers came into the picture, it was early June, and only one of the Hopple children was living at home. Donald, a little boy of six with large wondering eyes, was chauffeured daily to a private school in the next county. John was attending a military academy in Ohio, and Mary was enrolled in a girls' school in Virginia. Donald. John. Mary. The Hopples liked plain, honest names rooted in tradition.

On their youngest child they lavished affection and attention as well as playthings intended to shape his interests. He had his own computer and telescope and video library, his child-size guitar and golf clubs, his little NASA space suit. To the great concern of his father, none of these appealed to Donald in the least. His chief joy was romping with the assorted cats in the stable and telling them bedtime stories.

The subject was discussed one Friday evening in early June. Mr. Hopple had just flown in from Chicago, following a ten-day business trip to the Orient. In his London-tailored worsted, his custom-made wing tips, and his realistic toupee, he looked every inch the successful entrepreneur. The Jeep was waiting for him in the meadow, and his wife greeted him happily and affectionately, while his son jumped up and down with excitement and asked to carry his briefcase.

Then, while little Donald showered and dressed for dinner, his parents enjoyed their Quiet Hour in the master suite. Mr. Hopple, wearing a silk dressing gown, opened an enormous Dutch cupboard said to have belonged to Peter Stuyvesant, and now outfitted as a bar. "Will you have the usual, sweetheart?" he asked.

"Don't you think the occasion calls for champagne, darling?" his wife replied. "I'm so happy to see you safely home. There's a bottle of D.P. chilling in the refrigerator."

Her husband poured the champagne and proposed a sentimental toast to his lovely wife. Mrs. Hopple had been a national beauty queen twenty years before and still looked the part, whether wearing a Paris original to a charity ball or designer jeans around the farm.

"First tell me about the small fry," Mr. Hopple said. "They've been on my mind all week." The Hopples never called their children "kids."

"Good news from John," said his wife, looking radiant. "He's won two more honors in math and has made the golf team. He wants to attend a math camp this summer, but first he'd like to bring five schoolmates home for a week of fishing and shooting."

"Good boy! He has a well-balanced perspective. Is he interested in girls as yet?"

"I don't think so, dear. He's only ten, you know. Mary is having her first date this weekend, and it's with an ambassador's son—"

"From which country?" Mr. Hopple cut in quickly.

"Something South American, I believe. By the way, she's won all kinds of equestrian ribbons this spring, and she wants our permission to play polo. Her grades are excellent. She's beginning to talk about Harvard—and business administration."

"Good girl! Someday it will be Hopple & Daughter, Inc. And how is Donald progressing?"

Mrs. Hopple glowed with pleasure. "His teacher says he's three years ahead of his age group in reading, and he has a vivid imagination. We may have a writer in the family, dear. Donald is always making up little stories."

Mr. Hopple shook his head regretfully. "I had hoped for something better than that for Donald. How much time does he spend with his computer and his telescope?"

"None at all, I'm afraid, but I don't press him. He's such a bright, conscientious child, and so good! Cats are his chief interest right now. The calico in the stable had a litter last month, you remember, and Donald acts like a doting godfather. Sometimes I think that he may be headed for veterinary medicine."

"I hardly relish the prospect of introducing 'my son the horse doctor.' I'd rather have a writer in the family." Mr. Hopple poured champagne again. "And how is the household running, dear?"

"The week was rather eventful, darling. I've made a list. First, it appears there was a power outage Wednesday night; all the electric clocks were forty-seven minutes slow on Thursday morning. There was no storm to account for it. I wish there had been. We need rain badly. Ever since the outage, television reception has been poor. The repairman checked all our receivers and can find nothing wrong. The staff is quite upset. The houseman blames it on secret nuclear testing."

"And how is the staff otherwise?" The Hopples never referred to "servants."

"There are several developments. Both maids have announced that they're pregnant. . . . I've had to dismiss the stableboy because of his bad language. . . . And the cook is demanding more fringe benefits."

"Give her whatever she asks," Mr. Hopple said. "We don't want to lose Suzette. I trust the gardeners are well and happy."

Mrs. Hopple referred to her list. "Mr. Bunsen's arthritis is somewhat worse. We should hire another helper for him."

"Hire two. He's a loyal employee," her husband said. "Is the new houseman satisfactory?"

"I have only one complaint. When he drives Donald to school he alarms the boy with nonsense about Russian plots and visitors from outer space and poisons in our food."

"I'll speak to the man immediately. Were you able to replace the stableboy?"

"Happily, yes. The school principal sent me a senior who speaks decently. He's well-mannered and has just won a statewide science competition. He may have a good influence on our son, dear. Today Donald wore his NASA suit for the first time."

"That's promising. What's the boy's name?"

"Bobbie Wynkopp. He lives in the little house beyond our south gate."

"Remind me to inquire, dear, if he's noticed any trespassers in the south meadow. I saw evidence of a bonfire when I came in for a landing this afternoon. I don't object to picnickers, but I don't want them to start grass fires in this dry weather."

A melodious bell rang, and the Hopples finished dressing and went downstairs to dinner.

Donald appeared at the table in his little white Italian silk suit, basking in his parents' approval and waiting eagerly for the conversation to be directed his way. After the maid had served the leeks vinaigrette, Mr. Hopple said: "Well, young man, have you had any adventures this week?"

"Yes, sir," the boy said, his large eyes sparkling. "I saw a weird cat in the stable." Elevated on two cushions, he attacked the leeks proficiently with his junior-size knife and fork, crafted to match the family's heirloom sterling. "I don't know where he came from. He's got long whiskers." Donald held up both hands to indicate roughly eighteen inches.

"That sounds like a fish story to me," said Mr. Hopple with a broad wink.

Donald smiled at his father's badinage. "It's true. He's too little to have such long whiskers. He's weird."

His mother said gently: "Young cats have long whiskers and large ears, darling. Then they grow up to match them."

Donald shook his head. "He's not a kitten, Mother. He acts grown-up. Sometimes his whiskers are long, and sometimes they're short. He's weird. I call him Whiskers."

"Imagine that!" his father said, striving to maintain a serious mien. "Retractable whiskers!"

Donald explained: "They get long when he's looking for something. He sticks his nose in everything. He's nosy."

"The word we use, darling, is *inquisitive*," his mother said gently.

"His whiskers light up in the dark," the boy went on with a sense of importance as his confidence grew. "When he's in a dark corner they're green like our computer screens. And his ears go round and round." Donald twirled his finger to suggest a spinning top. "That's how he flies. He goes straight up like a helicopter."

A swift glance passed between the adults. "This Mr. Whiskers is a clever fellow," said Mr. Hopple. "What color is he?"

Donald thought for a moment. "Sometimes he's blue. Most of the time he's green. I saw him turn purple yesterday. That's because he was mad."

"*Angry,* darling," his mother murmured. "And what does the new stableboy think of Whiskers?"

"Bobbie couldn't see him. Whiskers doesn't like big people. When he sees grown-ups he disappears. Whoof! Like that!"

Mrs. Hopple rang the bell for the next course. "And what kind of voice does this wonderful little animal have, dear? Does he scold like the Siamese or meow like the other cats?"

Donald considered his reply while he properly chewed and swallowed the last mouthful of leek. Then he erupted into a loud babel of sounds: "AWK AWK ngngngngng hhhhhhhhh-hhhhhh beep-beep-beep beep-beep-beep AWK."

The maid's eyes expressed alarm as she entered the dining room to remove the plates, and she was still regarding Donald with suspicion when she served the next course.

At that moment the boy shouted: "There he is! There's Whiskers!" He pointed to the window, but by the time the adults had turned their heads to look, Whiskers had disappeared.

The main course was the kind of simple provincial dish the Hopples approved: a medley of white beans, lamb, pork ribs, homemade sausages, herbs, and a little potted pheasant. Their cook, imported from the French wine country, would have nothing to do with microwave ovens or food processors, so they had built a primitive kitchen with a walk-in fireplace to keep Suzette happy. The cassoulet that was now served had been simmering in the brick oven all day. With it came a change of subject matter, and the meal ended without further reference to Whiskers.

After dinner Donald performed his regular chore of feeding the Gang—taking their dinner tray upstairs in the glass-enclosed elevator, rinsing their antique silver drinking bowl (attributed to Paul Revere), and filling it with bottled water. Meanwhile his parents were served their coffee in the library.

"You were right about the boy," Mr. Hopple

remarked. "His imagination runs away with him."

His wife said: "Donald's story is probably an elaboration on an actual occurrence. No doubt the cat is a stray, perhaps the runt of a litter, unwanted, and thrown out of a passing car."

"You have an explanation for everything, sweetheart. And you are so efficient. Did you make any plans for the weekend?"

"No, darling. I knew you'd be coping with jet lag. But I invited the gardener's grandchildren to have lunch with Donald. They're his own age, and he needs to meet town children occasionally."

On Saturdays the Hopples usually breakfasted in festive style in the conservatory, but both maids were suffering from morning sickness the next day, so the family trooped into the kitchen. There they sat at an ancient wooden table from a French monastery, under a canopy of copper pots and drying herbs, while Suzette cooked an omelette in a long-handled copper skillet over an open fire.

After breakfast Donald said: "Mother, can I take some of the Gang's catfood to the kittens in the stable?"

"*May I,* darling," she corrected softly. "Yes,

you may, but ask yourself if it's advisable to spoil them. After all, they're only barn cats."

"Two of the kittens are very smart, Mother. They're as smart as the Siamese."

"All right, Donald. I value your opinion." After he had scampered away, Mrs. Hopple said to her husband: "See? The Whiskers story was only a fantasy. He's forgotten about it already. . . . By the way, don't forget to ask Bobbie about the bonfire, dear."

Her husband thanked her for the reminder and went to buzz the stable on the intercom. "Good morning, Bobbie. This is Hopple speaking. We haven't met as yet, but I've heard good reports of you."

"Thank you, sir."

"Since you live near the south gate, I'm wondering if you've observed any trespassing in the meadow. Someone had a bonfire there, and that's bad business."

"No, sir. Never saw anything like that," the new stableboy said, "but I've been away for three days at a science conference, you know."

"If you notice any unauthorized activity, please telephone us immediately—any hour of the day or evening."

"Sure thing," said Bobbie.

"One more question: Have you seen

any . . . *unusual* cats in the stable or on the grounds?"

"Only a bunch of kittens and an old mother cat."

"No strange-looking stray with long whiskers?"

There was a pause, and then the young man said: "No, I only heard some funny noises—like a duck quacking, and then some kind of electronic beep. I couldn't figure where it came from."

"Thank you, Bobbie. Keep up the good work."

Mr. Hopple flicked off the intercom and said to his wife: "Donald is making those ridiculous noises in the stable. How long should we allow this to go on before consulting the doctor?"

"Darling, he's just playing games. He'll grow out of it soon. It's common for young children to invent imaginary friends and have conversations with them."

"I can assure you that *I* never did," said her husband, and he went to his study, asking not to be disturbed.

Before noon the houseman took the Mercedes into town to pick up the Bunsen twins, a boy and a girl. Mrs. Hopple welcomed them warmly and gave them a picnic basket in which the cook had packed food enough for twelve children. "Wear your beeper, Donald darling," she reminded him. "I'll let you know when it's time to bring your guests back."

Donald drove the twins to the meadow in the pony cart. Having observed his father in social situations, he played the role of host nicely, and the picnic went smoothly. No one fell down. No one picked a fight. No one got sick.

When Mrs. Hopple beeped her son, he drove his guests back to the house with brief detours to the dog kennel, rabbit hutch, chicken coop, and horse stable.

"Did you have a nice time?" Mrs. Hopple asked the excited twins.

"I ate four chocolate things," said the boy.

"My mother told me to say thank you," said the girl.

"I saw a snake," the boy said.

"We saw Whiskers," the girl said.

"He's green!"

"No, he's blue with green whiskers."

"His eyes light up."

"Sparks come out of his whiskers."

"He can fly."

"Really?" said Donald's mother. "Did he say anything to you?"

The twins looked at each other. Then the boy

quacked like a duck, and the girl said: "Beep beep beep!"

Mrs. Hopple thought: Donald has coached them! Still, the mention of sparks made her uneasy. Living so far from town, the Hopples had an understandable fear of fire. She left the house hurriedly and rode a moped to the stable.

Bobbie was in the corral, exercising the horses. Donald was unhitching the pony. The barn cats were in evidence, but there was no sign of a creature with red-hot whiskers. Her usual buoyant spirit returned, and she laughed at herself for being gullible.

On the way back to the house she overtook the head gardener, laboring arthritically up the hill, carrying a basket of tulips and daffodils. She rebuked him kindly. "Mr. Bunsen, why didn't you send the flowers up with one of the boys?"

"Gotta keep movin'," he said, "or the old joints turn to *ce*—ment."

"Mr. Hopple is arranging to hire some more help for you."

"Well, 'twon't do no good. Nobody wants to do any work these days."

"By the way, you have two delightful grandchildren, Mr. Bunsen. It was a pleasure to have them visit us."

"They watch too much TV," he complained. . . . "Lookit that grass turnin" brown. No rain for ten days! . . . Somethin' else, too. Some kind of critter's been gettin' in the greenhouse. Eats the buds off the geraniums. And now the tractor's broke. Don't know what happened. Just conked out this afternoon."

"You must call the mechanic early Monday morning," Mrs. Hopple said encouragingly. "Ask for priority service."

"Well, 'twon't make no difference. They come when they feel like it."

The gardener's grouchy outlook had no effect on Mrs. Hopple, who was always cheerful. Mentally reciting a few lines of Wordsworth, she carried the flowers into the potting shed, a room entirely lined with ceramic tile. There she was selecting vases from a collection of fifty or more when a commotion in the nearby kitchen sent her hurrying to investigate.

Suzette was standing in the fireplace—which was now cold and swept clean—and she was banging pots and pans and screaming up the chimney. From the cook's raving—three parts English and two parts French—it appeared that a *diable* up on the *toit* was trying to get down the *cheminée* into the *cuisine*.

Mrs. Hopple commended the cook on her

bravery in driving a devil off the roof but assured her that the chimney was securely screened and nothing could possibly enter the kitchen by that route, whether a raccoon or squirrel or field mouse or devil.

Back in the potting shed she found a silver champagne bucket for the red tulips and was choosing something for the daffodils, when the buzzing intercom interrupted.

"Tractor's okay, Miz Hopple," said the gardener. "Started up again all by itself. But there's some glass busted out in the greenhouse."

She thanked Mr. Bunsen and went back to her flowers, smiling at the man's perverse habit of tempering good news with a bit of bad. As she was arranging daffodils in a copper jug, Donald burst into the potting shed. "I couldn't find you, Mother," he said in great distress. "The rabbits are gone! I think somebody stole them!"

"No, dear," she replied calmly. "I think you'll find them in the greenhouse, gorging on geranium buds. Now, how would you like strawberries Chantilly tonight?" It was the family's favorite dessert, and Donald jumped up and down and gave his mother a hug.

Later, she said to Suzette, speaking the cook's special language: "I'll drive to the *ferme* and pick up the *fraises* and the *crème*." Mrs. Hopple liked an excuse to breeze around the country roads in the Ferrari convertible with the top down. Today she would drive to the strawberry farm for freshly picked fruit and to the dairy farm for heavy cream.

First she ran upstairs to find a scarf for her hair. As she passed the door of the Gang's suite, she heard Donald making his ridiculous noises and the cats replying with yowling and mewing. She put her hand on the doorknob, then decided not to embarrass her son by intruding.

When she returned a moment later, silk-scarved and cashmere-sweatered, Donald was leaving the suite, looking pleased with himself.

"Are you having fun, darling?" she asked.

"Whiskers was in there," he replied. "He was climbing around the waterwheel, and he looked in the window. I let him in. He likes our cats a lot."

"He likes them *very much*, darling. I hope you closed the window again. We don't want the Gang to get out, do we?"

Blithely Mrs. Hopple went to the garage and slipped into the seat of the Ferrari. She pressed a button to lift the garage door and turned the key in the ignition. Nothing happened. There was not even a cough from the motor and not even a shudder from the big door. She persevered. She used sheer willpower. Nothing happened.

The houseman had not returned with the Mercedes after taking the twins home, but there were three other cars. She climbed into the Rolls; it would not start. The Caddy was equally dead. So was the Jeep.

Something, she thought, is mysteriously wrong. The houseman would blame it on the KGB or acid rain.

Resolutely she marched back to the house and confronted her husband in his study, where he was locked in with computer, briefcase, and dictating machine. He listened to her incredible story, sighed, then went to inspect the situation, while Mrs. Hopple did a few deep-breathing exercises to restore her equanimity.

"Nothing wrong," he said when he returned. "The cars start, and the doors open. I think you need a change of scene, sweetheart. We'll go out to dinner tonight. Wear your new Saint Laurent, and we'll go to the club. Suzette can give the boy his dinner."

"We can't, darling. We're having strawberries Chantilly, and I promised Donald."

So the Hopples stayed home and enjoyed an old-fashioned family evening. Dinner was served on the terrace, followed by croquet on the lawn and corn-popping over hot coals in the outdoor fireplace. Donald made no mention of Whiskers, and his parents made no inquiries.

Early Sunday morning, when the June sunrise and chattering birds were trying to rouse everyone at an abnormal hour, the telephone rang at Hopplewood Farm.

Mr. Hopple rose sleepily on an elbow and squinted at the digital clock radio. "Four-thirty! Who would call at this ungodly hour?"

Mrs. Hopple sat up in bed. "It's five twenty-five by the old clock on the mantel. There's been another power failure."

Her husband cleared his throat and picked up the receiver. "Yes?"

"Hi, Mr. Hopple. This is Bobbie Wynkopp. Sorry to call so early, but you told me—if I saw anything . . ."

"Yes, Bobbie. What is it?"

"That place in the meadow that was burned—how big was it?"

"Hmm . . . as well as I could estimate from the air . . . it was . . . about ten feet in diameter. A circular patch."

"Well, there's another one just like it."

"What! Did you see any trespassing?" Mr. Hopple was fully awake now.

There was a pause. "Mr. Hopple, you're not

gonna believe this, but last night I woke up because my room was all lit up. I sleep in the attic, on the side near the meadow, you know. It was kind of a green light. I looked out the window. . . . You're not gonna believe this, Mr. Hopple."

"Go ahead, Bobbie—please."

"Well, there was this aircraft coming down. Not like your kind of plane, Mr. Hopple. It was round, like a Frisbee. It came straight down—very slow, very quiet, you know. And it gave off a lot of light."

"If you're suggesting a flying saucer, Bobbie, I say you've been dreaming—or hallucinating."

"I was wide awake, sir. I swear! And I don't smoke. Ask anyone."

"Go on, Bobbie."

"The funny thing was . . . it was so *small!* Too small to carry a crew, you know, unless they happened to be like ten inches high. It landed, and there was some kind of activity around it. I couldn't see exactly. There was a fog rising over the meadow. So I ran downstairs to get my dad's binoculars. They were hard to find in the dark. The lights wouldn't go on. We were blacked out, you know. . . . Are you still there, Mr. Hopple?"

"I'm listening. What about your parents? Did they see the aircraft?"

"No, but I wish they had. Then I wouldn't sound like some kind of crazy. My mother works nights at the hospital, and when Dad goes to bed, he flakes right out."

"What did you see with the binoculars?"

"I was too late. They were taking off. The thing rose straight up—very slow, you know. And when it got up there . . . ZIP! It disappeared. No kidding. I couldn't sleep after that. When it got halfway daylight I went out to the meadow and had a look. The thing scorched a circle, about ten feet across. You can see for yourself. Maybe you should have it tested for radioactivity or something. Maybe I shouldn't have gone near it, you know."

"Thank you, Bobbie. That's an extremely interesting account. We'll discuss it further, after I've made some inquiries. Meanwhile, I'd consider it classified information if I were you."

"Classified! Don't worry, Mr. Hopple."

"Was that the stableboy?" his wife asked. "Is anything wrong? . . . *Darling, is anything wrong?*"

Mr. Hopple had walked to the south window and was gazing in the direction of the meadow—a study in preoccupation. "I beg your pardon. What did you say? That boy told me a wild story. . . . Ten-foot diameter! He's right; that's remarkably small."

There was a loud thump as a six-year-old threw himself against the bedroom door and hurtled into the room.

"Darling," his mother reminded him, "we always knock before entering."

"They're gone! They're gone!" he shouted in a childish treble. "I wanted to say good morning, and they're not there!"

"*Who's* not there, darling?"

"The Gang! They got out the window and climbed down the waterwheel!"

"Donald! Did you leave the window open?"

"No, Mother. The window's *broke*. Broken," he added, catching his mother's eye. "The glass is kind of . . . *melted!* I think Whiskers did it. He kidnapped them!"

She shooed him out of the bedroom. "Go and get dressed, dear. We'll find the Gang. We'll organize a search party."

Mrs. Hopple slipped into a peignoir and left the suite. When she returned, a moment later, her husband was still staring into space at the south window. "Donald's right," she said. "The glass has actually been *melted*. How very strange!"

Still Mr. Hopple stared, as if in a trance.

"Dearest, are you all right? Did you hear what Donald said?"

Her husband stirred himself and walked away from the window. He said: "You can organize a search party if you wish, but you'll never find the Gang. They're not coming back. Neither is Whiskers."

He was right. They never came back. The two smartest kittens in the stable also disappeared that night, according to Donald, but the rabbits were found in the greenhouse, having the time of their lives.

Life at Hopplewood Farm is quite ordinary now. Garage doors open. Cars start. Television reception is perfect. Only during severe electrical storms does the power fail. No one lets the rabbits out of the hutch. The tractor is entirely reliable. Nothing tries to sneak down the chimney. Window glass never melts.

And little Donald, who may suspect more than he's telling, discusses planets and asteroids at the dinner table and spends hours peering through his telescope when his parents think he's asleep.

The Sin of Madame Phloi

From the very beginning Madame Phloi felt an instinctive distaste for the man who moved into the apartment next door. He was fat, and his trouser cuffs had the unsavory odor of fire hydrant.

They met for the first time in the decrepit elevator as it lurched up to the tenth floor of the

"The Sin of Madame Phloi" was first published in *Ellery Queen's Mystery Magazine*, June 1962.

old building, once fashionable but now coming apart at the seams. Madame Phloi had been out for a stroll in the city park, chewing city grass and chasing faded butterflies, and as she and her companion stepped on the elevator for the slow ride upward, the car was already half-filled with the new neighbor.

The fat man and the Madame presented a contrast that was not unusual in this apartment house, which had a brilliant past and no future. He was bulky, uncouth, sloppily attired. Madame Phloi was a long-legged blue-eyed aristocrat whose creamy fawn coat shaded to brown at the extremities.

The Madame deplored fat men. They had no laps, and of what use is a lapless human? Nevertheless, she gave him the common courtesy of a sniff at his trouser cuffs and immediately backed away, twitching her nose and showing her teeth.

"*GET* that cat away from me," the fat man roared, stamping his feet thunderously at Madame Phloi. Her companion pulled the leash although there was no need; the Madame with one backward leap had retreated to a safe corner of the elevator, which shuddered and continued its groaning ascent.

The Sin of Madame Phloi

"Don't you like animals?" inquired the gentle voice at the other end of the leash.

"Filthy, sneaky beasts," the fat man said with a snarl. "Last place I lived, some lousy cat got in my room and et my parakeet."

"I'm sorry to hear that. But you don't need to worry about Madame Phloi and Thapthim. They never leave the apartment except on a leash."

"You got TWO? Well, keep 'em away from me or I'll break their rotten necks. I ain't wrung a cat's neck since I was fourteen, but I remember how."

And with the long black box he was carrying, the fat man lunged at the impeccable Madame Phloi, who sat in her corner, flat eared and tense. Her fur bristled, and she tried to dart away. Even when her companion picked her up in protective arms, Madame Phloi's body was taut and trembling.

Not until she was safely home in her modest but well-cushioned apartment did she relax. She walked stiff-legged to the sunny spot on the carpet where Thapthim was sleeping and licked the top of his head. Then she had a complete bath herself—to rid her coat of the fat man's odor. Thapthim did not wake.

This drowsy, unambitious, amiable creature—her son—was a puzzle to Madame Phloi; she herself was sensitive and spirited. She didn't try to understand him; she merely loved him. She spent hours washing his paws and breast and other parts he could easily have reached with his own tongue. At dinnertime she consumed her food slowly so there would be something left on her plate for his dessert, and he always gobbled the extra portion hungrily. And when he slept, which was most of the time, she kept watch by his side, sitting with a tall regal posture until she swayed with weariness. Then she made herself into a small bundle and dozed with one eye open.

Thapthim was lovable, to be sure. He appealed to other cats, large and small dogs, people, and even ailurophobes in a limited way. He had a face like a beautiful brown flower and large blue eyes, tender and trusting. Ever since he was a kitten he had been willing to purr at the touch of a hand—any hand. Eventually he became so agreeable that he purred if anyone looked in his direction from across the room. What's more, he came when called; he gratefully devoured whatever was served on his dinner plate; and when he was told to get down, he got down.

His wise parent disapproved of this uncatly

conduct; it indicated a certain lack of character, and no good would come of it. By her own example she tried to guide him. When dinner was served she gave the plate a haughty sniff and walked away, no matter how tempting the dish. That was the way it was done by any self-respecting feline. In a minute or two she returned and condescended to dine, but never with open enthusiasm.

Furthermore, when human hands reached out, the catly thing was to bound away, lead them a chase, flirt a little before allowing oneself to be caught and cuddled. Thapthim, sorry to say, greeted any friendly overture by rolling over, purring, and looking soulful.

From an early age he had known the rules of the apartment:

"No sleeping in the cupboard with the pots and pans."

"Sitting on the table with the typewriter is permissible."

"Sitting on the table with the coffeepot is never allowed."

The sad truth was that Thapthim obeyed these rules. Madame Phloi, on the other hand, knew that a rule was a challenge, and it was a matter of integrity to violate it. To obey was to sacrifice one's dignity. . . . It seemed that her son would never learn the true values in life.

To be sure, Thapthim was adored for his good nature in the human world of typewriters and coffeepots. But Madame Phloi was equally adored—and for the correct reasons. She was respected for her independence, admired for her clever methods of getting her own way, and loved for the cowlick on her white breast and the squint in her delphinium blue eyes. In appearance and behavior she was a classic Siamese. By cocking her head and staring with heart-melting eyes, she could charm a porterhouse steak out from under a knife and fork.

Until the fat man and his black box moved in next door, Madame Phloi had never known an unfriendly soul. She had two companions in her tenth-floor apartment—genial creatures without names who came and went a good deal. One was an easy mark for between-meal snacks; a tap on his ankle always produced a crunchy tidbit. The other served as a hot-water bottle on cold nights and punctually obliged whenever the Madame wished to have her underside stroked or her cheekbones massaged.

Life was not all petting and treats, however; Madame Phloi had her regular work. She was official watcher and listener for the household.

The Sin of Madame Phloi

There were six windows that required watching, for a wide ledge ran around the building flush with the tenth-floor windowsills, and this was a promenade for pigeons. They strutted, searched their feathers, and ignored the Madame, who sat on the sill and watched them dispassionately but thoroughly through the window screen.

While watching was a daytime job, listening was done after dark, requiring greater concentration. Madame Phloi listened for noises in the walls. She heard termites chewing, pipes sweating, and sometimes the ancient plaster cracking, but mostly she listened to the ghosts of generations of deceased mice.

One evening, shortly after the incident in the elevator, Madame Phloi was listening. Thapthim was sleeping, and the other two were quietly turning pages of books, when a strange and horrendous sound came from the wall. The Madame's ears flicked to attention, then flattened against her head.

An interminable screech was coming out of that wall, like nothing the Madame had ever heard. It chilled the blood and tortured the ears. So painful was the shrillness that Madame Phloi threw back her head and complained with a piercing howl of her own. The strident din even waked Thapthim. He looked about in alarm, shook his head wildly, and clawed at his ears to get rid of the offending noise.

The others heard it, too.

"Listen to that!" said the one with the gentle voice.

"It must be the new man next door," said the other. "It's incredible!"

"How could anyone so crude produce anything so exquisite? Is it Prokofiev he's playing?"

"I think it's Bartók."

"He was carrying his violin in the elevator today. He tried to hit Phloi with it."

"He's a nut. . . . Look at the cats! Apparently they don't care for violin music."

Madame Phloi and Thapthim, bounding from the room, collided with each other in a rush to hide under the bed.

That was not the only noise emanating from the next-door apartment in those upsetting days after the fat man moved in. The following evening, when Madame Phloi walked into the living room to commence her listening, she heard a fluttering sound dimly through the wall, accompanied by highly conversational chirping. This was agreeable music, and she settled down on the sofa to enjoy it, tucking her brown paws neatly under her creamy body.

Her contentment was soon disturbed, however, by a slamming door and then the fat man's voice bursting through the wall like thunder.

"Look what you done, you dirty skunk!" he bellowed. "Right in my fiddle! Get back in your cage before I brain you!"

There was a frantic beating of wings.

"*GET* down off that window or I'll bash your head in!"

The threat brought a torrent of chirping.

"Shut up, you stupid cluck! Shut up and get back in that cage or I'll . . ."

There was a splintering crash, and then all was quiet except for an occasional pitiful "peep!"

Madame Phloi was fascinated. In fact, when she resumed her watching chore the next day, pigeons seemed rather insipid entertainment. Thapthim was asleep, and the others had left for the day, but not before opening the window and placing a small cushion on the chilly marble sill.

There she sat, a small but alert package of fur, sniffing the welcome summer air, seeing all and knowing all. She knew, for example, that the person walking down the tenth-floor hallway, wearing old tennis shoes and limping slightly, would halt at the door, set down his pail, and let himself in with a passkey.

Indeed, she hardly bothered to turn her head when the window washer entered. He was one of her regular court of admirers. His odor was friendly, although it suggested damp basements and floor mops, and he talked sensibly; there was none of that falsetto foolishness with which some persons insulted the Madame's intelligence.

"Hop down, kitty," he said in a musical voice. "Charlie's gotta take out that screen. See, I brought some cheese for the pretty kitty."

He held out a modest offering of rat cheese, and Madame Phloi investigated it and found it was the wrong variety, and she shook one fastidious paw at it.

"Mighty fussy cat," Charlie laughed. "Well, now, you sit there and watch Charlie clean this here window. Don't you go jumpin' out on the ledge, 'cause Charlie ain't runnin' after you. No sir! That old ledge, she's startin' to crumble. Someday them pigeons'll stamp their feet hard, and down she goes! . . . Hey, lookit the broken glass out here! Somebody busted a window."

The Sin of Madame Phloi

Charlie sat on the marble sill and pulled the upper sash down in his lap, and while Madame Phloi followed his movements carefully, Thapthim sauntered into the room, yawning and stretching, and swallowed the cheese.

"Now Charlie puts the screen back in, and you two guys can watch them crazy pigeons some more. This screen, she's comin' apart, too. Whole buildin's crackin' up."

Remembering to replace the cushion on the cool, hard sill, he went on to clean the remaining windows, and the Madame resumed her post, sitting on the edge of the cushion so that Thapthim could have most of it.

The pigeons were late that morning, probably frightened away by the window washer. When the first visitor skimmed in on a blue gray wing, Madame Phloi first noticed the tiny opening in the screen. Every aperture, no matter how small, was a temptation; she had to prove she could wriggle through any tight space, whether there was a good reason or not.

She waited until Charlie had limped out of the apartment before she started pushing at the screen with her nose, first gingerly, then stubbornly. Inch by inch the rusted mesh ripped away from the frame until the whole corner formed a loose flap. Then Madame Phloi slithered through—nose and ears, slender shoulders, dainty Queen Anne forefeet, svelte torso, lean flanks, hind legs like steel springs, and finally proud brown tail. For the first time in her life she found herself on the pigeon promenade. She shuddered deliciously.

Inside the screen the lethargic Thapthim, jolted by this strange turn of affairs, watched his daring parent with a quarter inch of his pink tongue protruding. They touched noses briefly through the screen, and the Madame proceeded to explore. She advanced cautiously and with mincing step, for the pigeons had not been tidy in their habits.

The ledge was about two feet wide. Moving warily, Madame Phloi advanced to its edge, nose down and tail high. Ten stories below there were moving objects but nothing of interest, she decided. She walked daintily along the extreme edge to avoid the broken glass, venturing in the direction of the fat man's apartment, impelled by some half-forgotten curiosity.

His window stood open and unscreened, and Madame Phloi peered in politely. There, sprawled on the floor, lay the fat man himself, snorting and heaving his immense paunch in a kind of rhythm. It always alarmed her to see a human on the floor, which she considered feline domain. She licked her nose apprehensively and stared at him with enormous eyes. In a dark corner of the room something fluttered and squawked, and the fat man opened his eyes.

"SHcrrff! *GET* out of here!" he shouted, struggling to his feet and shaking his fist at the window.

In three leaps Madame Phloi crossed the ledge back to her own window and pushed through the screen to safety. After looking back to see if the fat man might be chasing her and being reassured that he was not, she washed Thapthim's ears and her own paws and sat down to wait for pigeons.

Like any normal cat Madame Phloi lived by the Rule of Three. She resisted any innovation three times before accepting it, tackled an obstacle three times before giving up, and tried each activity three times before tiring of it. Consequently she made two more sallies to the pigeon promenade and eventually convinced Thapthim to join her.

Together they peered over the edge at the world below. The sense of freedom was intoxicating. Recklessly Thapthim made a leap at a low-flying pigeon and landed on his mother's back. She cuffed his ear in retaliation. He poked her nose. They grappled and rolled over and over on the ledge, oblivious of the long drop below them, taking playful nips of each other's hide and snarling gutteral expressions of glee.

Suddenly Madame Phloi scrambled to her feet and crouched in a defensive position. The fat man was leaning from his window.

"Here, kitty, kitty," he was saying in one of those despised falsetto voices, offering some bit of food in a saucer. The Madame froze, but Thapthim turned his beautiful trusting eyes on the stranger and advanced along the ledge. Purring and waving his tail cordially, he walked into the trap. It all happened in a matter of seconds: the saucer was withdrawn and a long black box was swung at Thapthim like a baseball bat, sweeping him off the ledge and into space. He was silent as he fell.

When the family came home, laughing and chattering, with their arms full of packages, they knew at once something was amiss. No one greeted them at the door. Madame Phloi hunched moodily on the windowsill, staring at a hole in the screen, and Thapthim was not to be found.

"The screen's torn!" cried the gentle voice.

"I'll bet he's out on the ledge."

The Sin of Madame Phloi

"Can you lean out and look? Be careful."

"You hold Phloi."

"Can you see him?"

"Not a sign of him! There's a lot of glass scattered around, and the window next door is broken."

"Do you suppose that man . . . ? I feel sick."

"Don't worry, dear. We'll find him. . . . There's the doorbell! Maybe someone's bringing him home."

It was Charlie standing at the door, fidgeting uncomfortably. " 'Scuse me, folks," he said. "You missin' one of your kitties?"

"Yes! Have you found him?"

"Poor little guy," said Charlie. "Found him lyin' right under your window, where the bushes is thick."

"He's dead!" the gentle one moaned.

"Yes, ma'am. That's a long way down."

"Where is he now?"

"I got him down in the basement, ma'am. I'll take care of him real nice. I don't think you'd want to see the poor guy."

Still Madame Phloi stared at the hole in the screen and waited for Thapthim. From time to time she checked the other windows, just to be sure. As time passed and he did not return, she looked behind the radiators and under the bed.

She pried open cupboard doors and tried to burrow her way into closets. She sniffed all around the front door. Finally she stood in the middle of the living room and called loudly in a high-pitched, wailing voice.

Later that evening Charlie paid another visit to the apartment.

"Only wanted to tell you, ma'am, how nice I took care of him," he said. "I got a box that was just the right size—a white box, it was, from one of the nice stores. And I wrapped him up in some old blue curtain. It looked real pretty with his fur. And I buried the little guy right under your windows, behind the bushes.

And still Madame Phloi searched, returning again and again to watch the ledge from which Thapthim had disappeared. She scorned food. She rebuffed any attempts at consolation. And all night she sat wide-eyed and waiting in the dark.

The living room window was now tightly closed, but the following day the Madame—when she was left by herself in the lonely apartment—went to work on the bedroom screens. One was new and hopeless, but the second screen was slightly corroded, and she was soon nosing through a slit that lengthened as she struggled out onto the ledge.

The Sin of Madame Phloi

Picking her way through the broken glass, she approached the spot where Thapthim had vanished. And then it all happened again. There he was—the fat man—holding out a saucer.

"Here, kitty, kitty."

Madame Phloi hunched down and backed away.

"Kitty want some milk?" It was that ugly falsetto, but she did not run home this time. She crouched on the ledge, a few inches out of his reach.

"Nice kitty. Nice kitty."

Madame Phloi crept with caution toward the saucer in the outstretched fist, and stealthily the fat man extended another hand, snapping his fingers as one would do to call a dog.

The Madame retreated diagonally—half toward home and half toward the dangerous brink.

"Here, kitty. Nice kitty," he cooed, leaning farther out of his window, but under his breath he muttered: "You dirty sneak! I'll get you if it's the last thing I ever do. Comin' after my bird, weren't you?"

Madame Phloi recognized danger with all her senses. Her ears were back, her whiskers curled, and her white underside hugged the ledge.

A little closer she moved, and the fat man made a grab for her. She jerked back a step, with unblinking eyes fixed on his sweating face. He was furtively laying the saucer aside, she noticed, and edging his fat paunch farther out the window.

Once more she advanced almost into his grasp, and again he lunged at her with both of his powerful arms.

"This time I'll get you, you stinkin' cat," he mumbled, and raising one knee to the windowsill, he threw himself at Madame Phloi. As she slipped through his fingers, he landed on the ledge with all his weight.

A section of masonry crumbled beneath him. He bellowed, clutching at air, and at the same time a streak of creamy brown fur flashed out of sight.

The fat man was not silent as he fell.

As for Madame Phloi, she was found doubled in half—in a patch of sunshine on her living room carpet—innocently washing her fine brown tail.

Tragedy on New Year's Eve

January 1

Dear Tom,

Another New Year is beginning. I hope and
pray that the trouble will end soon, and you'll
be stationed closer to home. You are constantly
in my thoughts.

"Tragedy on New Year's Eve" was first published in *Ellery
Queen's Mystery Magazine*, March 1968.

It's four in the morning on New Year's Day—strange hour for a mother to be writing to her son—but I'm so upset, Tom dear. A terrible accident just happened behind our apartment building. I'm home alone—Jim is working—and I've got to tell somebody about it.

Jim went on special duty with the Cleanup Squad tonight, so I curled up on the sofa and read a mystery novel, and at midnight I opened the window and listened to the horns blowing and bells ringing. (Excuse the smudge. There's a cat sitting on the desk, pawing the paper as I write. Just a stray that I picked up.)

At midnight the neighborhood looked like a Christmas tree—green lights on the gas station—red neon on Wally's Tavern—traffic lights winking. The traffic was moving slowly—we'd had a freezing rain, then more snow—and I said a little prayer that Jim would get home safely.

After that I put on the pretty fleece robe he gave me for Christmas and had a snooze on the sofa, because I promised to wait up for him. The sirens kept waking me up—police, ambulance, fire—then I'd doze off again.

Suddenly loud noises jolted me awake. Bang—bang—CRASH—then shattering glass.

It came from the rear of the building. I ran to the kitchen window and looked out, and there was this black car—up over the sidewalk—rammed into the old brick warehouse back there. The car doors were flung open, and the interior light was on, and something dark was sprawled out of the driver's seat with the head hanging down in the snow. Man or woman? I couldn't tell.

I was stunned, but I knew enough to call the police. When I went back to the window everything down on the street was quiet as a morgue. No traffic. No one came running. No lights shining out of apartment windows. And there was this stranger hanging out of the wrecked car—dead or dying.

I thought about you, Tom, and how I'd feel if you were injured and alone like that, and I couldn't help crying. So I went downstairs to the street. Grabbed Jim's hunting jacket—ran down three flights—couldn't wait for the elevator—then out the back door where they park the dumpsters—and across the street.

It was a young man about your age, Tom, and I thought my heart would break. His head was covered with blood, and the snow was stained, and I knew he was dead. I couldn't leave him there alone, so I stayed and prayed a little until the flashing blue lights turned into the street.

There I was—standing in the snow in my slippers and robe and a hunting jacket, so I ran back to the building and watched from the shadow of the doorway.

An officer jumped out of the patrol car and yelled to his partner: "Radio for a wagon. This one's had it!"

And that's when I saw something moving in the darkness. At first I thought it was a horrid rat, like they've got in this neighborhood. Then this black cat darted out of the shadows and came right up to me, holding up one paw. It wanted to get in out of the snow. I picked it up—you know how much I like cats—and its feet were like ice. I was shivering, too, so we both came upstairs to get warm.

I watched from the window till they took the body away, and I couldn't help thinking of his poor mother—and how the police would knock on the door and take her downtown to the morgue. I wonder who he was. Maybe it will be in the newspaper.

I wish Jim would get home. The cat sits on my desk staring at me and throwing a shadow across the paper so I can't see what I'm writing. He's very sleek and black—with yellow eyes.

He must belong to someone in this building, but he's quite contented to stay here.

My mind keeps going back to that young man—drinking too much at some New Year's Eve party. Maybe he lived in this building and was coming home. I haven't met any of the neighbors. Jim says they're all kooks, and it's best if we stay to ourselves. The neighborhood is run-down, but the apartment is comfortable, and we're close to the precinct station.

When Jim retires next year we'll get a small house in Northport. I never thought I'd be married again—and to a detective! Remember how you and I used to read about Hercule Poirot and Inspector Maigret when we lived in Northport?

I hear Jim coming. Will finish this later.

New Year's afternoon

Here I am again. Jim's taking a nap. I told him about the accident, and he said: "Another drunk! He was asking for it."

He doesn't know I went downstairs in my robe and slippers, and it was hard to explain where the cat came from. It's still here—follows me around like a shadow.

There! I just heard it on the radio! First traffic fatality of the year—Wallace Sloan, 25, of 18309 Hamilton—car rammed into a brick building after hitting two utility poles.

They towed the wreck away, and now they're fixing the poles. I asked the superintendent if any tenant lost a black kitty, but he didn't know.

Dear son, take care. We pray you'll be home soon.

Love from Mother

January 4

Dear Tom,

Glad the fruitcake arrived in one piece. Are you getting decent food? Did you get my letter about the accident? Here's more news: When Jim heard the victim's name, he said: "That's the young guy that owns Wally's Tavern. It's a real dive."

Then I got the Monday paper and read the obituary. Wallace Sloan left a wife and four children! So young! My heart went out to the family. I know what it's like to be a widow with a young son. Imagine being left with four! That poor woman!

Tom, you may think this is strange, but—I went to the funeral. Jim thought I was going downtown to shop the January sales. It was terribly depressing—hardly any mourners—and the widow looked like a mere child! Outside the funeral home I got talking to a neighbor of the Sloans, and she said: "People think Wally was a drunk, but I'm telling you—he never touched liquor. He worked hard, day and night. Had to, I guess, with four kids to support—and another one on the way. Must have been dead tired and fell asleep at the wheel."

Very peculiar! You see, Tom, he was traveling east, evidently coming from the big lot behind the gas station, where the bar customers park. If he was cold sober, would he fall asleep after driving half a block? Not on that street! It's so full of frozen ruts, it shakes your teeth out!

Don't know why I'm so concerned. Probably because I read too many mystery stories. Do you have a chance to read, Tom? Shall I send you some paperbacks?

Well, anyway, I asked some questions at the grocery store, and I found out two things for sure. Wally Sloan always parked in the lot behind the gas station, AND he never took a drink.

The cat is still here, following me around. He must be lonely. I call him Shadow. I bought some catfood and fixed a toidy box for him. He doesn't want to go out—just stays close to me. Really a nice cat.

Now I must set the table for dinner. Jim has switched to the day shift. We're having your favorite meat loaf tonight. Will write again soon.

Love from Mother

January 5

Dear Tom,

I've been listening to the news bulletins and thanking God you're in the ground crew. Are you all right? Is there anything I can send you?

I must tell you the latest! Today I called on Wally Sloan's widow. I told her a fib—said I knew Wally at the tavern. I took her a home-made fruitcake and a large jar of my straw-berry jam, and she almost fainted. I guess city folks don't expect things like that. It's not like Northport.

I thought it might comfort her to know that

someone stood by on the night of the accident. When I told her, she squeezed my hand and then ran crying into the bedroom.

They have a nice house. Her mother was there, and I said: "Do you think your daughter will be able to manage?" I was thinking of the four little ones, you know.

"She'll manage all right," the mother said, kind of stern and angry, "but no thanks to him! He left nothing but debts."

"What a pity," I said. "Wally worked so hard."

She snorted. "Running a bar? What kind of work is that? He could've had a nice job downtown, but he'd rather mix with riffraff and spend his afternoons at the racetrack."

Aha, Dr. Watson! A new development! Now, we know Wally was a gambler! When I got home I tried to figure out a plan. The cat was hanging around, getting his nose into everything I tried to do, and I said to him: "Shadow, what would Miss Marple do in a case like this? What would Hildegarde Withers do?" Shadow always stares at me as if he knows what I'm saying—or he's trying to tell me something.

Well, after dinner, Jim went to his lodge meeting, and I started ringing doorbells in our building. At 408 an elderly man came to the door, and I said: "Excuse me, I'm your neighbor in 410. I picked up a stray cat on New Year's Eve and somebody said it might be yours. It's black."

"Our cat's ginger," he said, "and she's right there behind the radiator."

I rang about twenty doorbells. Some people said no and slammed the door, but most of the tenants were nice. We'd have a few pleasant words about the cat, and then I'd mention the accident. Quite a few knew Wally from going to the tavern.

At 503 a middle-aged woman came to the door, looking like a real floozy. She invited me in for a drink. Jim would have a fit if he knew I accepted, but all I drank was a tiny beer.

She said: "The blankety-blank tavern's closed now, and you gotta drink at home. It ain't no fun." Her eyes were sort of glassy, and her hair was a mess. "Too bad," she said. "Wally was a nice kid—and a big spender. I like big spenders."

"His bar business must have been very successful," I said.

She grinned at me. (Terrible teeth!) "You kidding? Wally had something going on the side. Don't we all?"

I said I understood he played the horses.

"Play 'em? Hell, he was a bookie! He'd lose his liquor license if they found out, so he kept it pretty quiet. Gus was his pickup man."

"Gus?"

"You know Gus—the mechanic at the gas station. He picked up bets for Wally. There was a big hassle at the bar New Year's Eve. Gus was slow with a payoff, and the guy tried to take it out of his hide."

"Was anyone hurt?"

"Gus got a shiner, that's all. Wally threw 'em both outa the bar. Can't blame Larry. He bet five hundred and the horse payed twenty-to-one."

"Larry?"

"You know Larry—on the third floor. Big guy. Male nurse at the hospital. Could've broke Gus in two."

Of course, I went right down to the lobby and looked at mailboxes. There was an L. Marcus in 311. I went up and rang his doorbell, but he wasn't home.

I wonder why Gus was slow in paying off. Twenty-to-one! Why, that's ten thousand, isn't it? Do you think Wally's accident had anything to do with that bet?

If I hear more, I'll write.

Love from Mother

P.S.

Now it's Friday. Didn't get a chance to mail this yesterday. This morning I was stroking Shadow and thinking about the accident, and I could recall the scene plain as day—everything black and white like an old movie. Black blood on the white snow—black warehouse—parked cars covered with white snow—black tire tracks where Wally's car went over the sidewalk—two black utility poles knocked over—even a black cat.

Then I remembered something about Wally's car. It was all black! Wouldn't it have some snow on the top or the hood if it had been parked in the open lot? Even the collision wouldn't knock it all off. It was freezing and snowing off and on all evening.

Tom, do you remember Uncle Roy's accident three years ago? Do you remember what caused it? Well, that gave me an idea, and I went to the gas station to talk to Gus. Jim rode to work with his partner this morning, so I took our car to the garage and told Gus the fan belt was making a funny noise. (Another fib.) Then I mentioned the accident. I said: "We all know Wally didn't drink. Maybe something went wrong with his car."

Gus said: "Yeah, he told me the steering was on the blink. I told him to leave it in the lot and gimme the keys and I'd fix it Monday. But I guess he tried to drive it home—crazy fool! We could've given him a loaner."

Then I told him about finding the mysterious black cat right after the accident.

He said: "Wally's kids—they got a black cat. Wally brought it to the bar sometimes when the rats got bad."

"Was the cat in the bar New Year's Eve?"

"I dunno," he said. "I wasn't there."

And yet there was a big yellow ring around his eye! "Oh, dear!" I said. "You got a bad poke in the eye, looks like."

"Yeah," he said. "Been playin' ice hockey."

That's all so far, Tom. Write when you can. I read your letters over and over.

Mother

January 9

Dear Tom,

A quick note to let you know my suspicions were correct! After dinner Friday night I said to

Jim: "Do you believe in Providence, dear? When Wally Slaon was killed, Providence arranged to have a detective's wife looking out the window—an old busybody who reads mystery stories." I said: "I think Wally Sloan was murdered. I think the garage mechanic loosened a steering knuckle on his car so Wally would lose control when it hit the first bump. You know Gus at the gas station? The police ought to pick him up for questioning. The woman in 503 might know something, too. Also a male nurse in 311."

Tom, I wish you could have seen the flabbergasted look on Jim's face.

That was Friday. Today the Homicide men got the whole story. Gus lost Larry's five hundred in a crap game—never placed the bet at all! Then Gus tried to wiggle out of the mess by blaming it on Wally. To cover up, he rigged Wally's car for the fatal accident.

There was no snow on that car, so I was sure it had been inside the garage, and on a crazy hunch I suspected Gus of tampering with it. Jim is very proud of me, and I hope you are, too, Tom dear.

Love from Mother

P.S.

Forgot to tell you. Shadow disappeared mysteriously Friday night. He got out somehow, and we haven't seen him since. It's almost as if he wanted to tell me something, and after the truth came out, he just vanished! Too bad. He was a nice cat. I liked him.